WHAT HAPPENS NEXT

Claire Swinarski

HARPER
An Imprint of HarperCollinsPublishers

What Happens Next

For information address HarperCollins Children's Books, a division of HarperCollins Publishers, 195 Broadway, New York, NY 10007.
www.harpercollinschildrens.com

Library of Congress Control Number: 2019951151
ISBN 978-0-06-291267-1

Typography by Catherine San Juan
20 21 22 23 24 PC/LSC 10 9 8 7 6 5 4 3 2 1

First Edition

For my sisters:

Ellen

Jenna

Asia

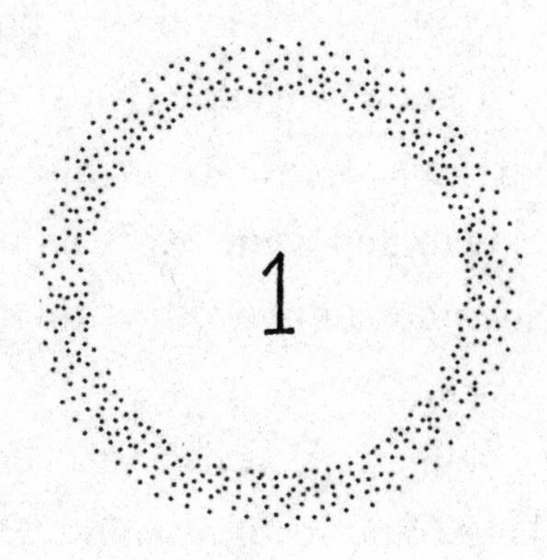

1

AUGUST, PRESENT DAY

Twelve years old

The night I saw Dr. Leo Lacamoire, I was looking at the stars.

"Abby! Did you take my sweatshirt?"

Lyra, the lyre. That's a fancy word for harp. Sagittarius, the archer.

"Abby, I know you can hear me. Sweatshirt. Now!"

Scorpius, the scorpion. That one was always tricky.

"*Abby!*"

Just as I located Delphinus, the dolphin, my sister burst into the attic, her hair falling out of her ponytail and into her eyes.

"I am going to be late to work if I don't leave *five minutes ago*, and I know you stole that sweatshirt." Jade was sixteen, four years older than me. She had blond hair with a purple streak and some boy's number scribbled on her palm. She popped popcorn at the movie theater three nights a week.

"I don't have your stupid sweatshirt." I did.

"You do!" Jade could read my mind. Or it was obvious. She was used to me being a liar. That's important to remember: sometimes, I lie.

"It's cold out," I whined. "Dad and I are going to the park tonight."

"I don't care if you're going to see Harry Styles! It's my *uniform*." The movie theater usually jacked the air-conditioning up so high, all the employees got thick fleeces to wear. I was always stealing Jade's. And her scarves, and her eyeliner, and anything else I could swipe. It was my sisterly duty, really.

"It's in my closet," I grumbled, and she stomped out. Jade and I shared a bedroom. Which was half the reason I spent most of my time in the attic. The other half was the stars.

My oldest sister, Blair, used to have her own room. Now it was empty. I didn't have to steal from her; she'd just let me borrow stuff. Jade would have kept a padlock on her closet if Mom let her.

Jade, again: "Dad says if you want to go, you need to get your butt downstairs. He's tired."

I peered into the telescope once more, to get one last glance at Delphinus. But my elbow had hit my telescope when I turned to talk to Jade. Instead of pointing me toward the night sky, it had swung down to Eagle's Nest, one of the nicest cabins my parents owned. It was right across the street from our house. So I didn't see the cluster of stars that someone had at one point thought resembled a sea creature. I saw one of the brightest stars in the entire universe—Dr. Leo Lacamoire himself, staring out across the lake that went on for miles.

But I didn't yet know that it was Dr. Leo Lacamoire. I didn't know why his gaze was fixed out on the water. I only knew that he looked like a man a little older than my dad, with a scratchy beard and pasty skin. I only knew that he seemed incredibly sad, and that now—

He was looking at me.

I ducked. Like a total idiot. Crap! *Not good, not good, not good.* I wasn't trying to be a snoop, but I clearly had a freaking *telescope* pointed at the guy's cabin. He was going to call the office and report a twelve-year-old creeper, and my mom would kill me.

Our family owned Camp McCourt—a bunch of cabins, a bar, and a dock—in Moose Junction, Wisconsin. Tourists came from all over the Midwest to hunt, fish, and see the stars at night. We'd had a few famous people visit over the years—the governor, some guy who had been in a handful of cheese commercials, and the couple that owned eighty-two frozen custard spots around the country who'd fought louder than firecrackers all weekend. Our fanciest guests stayed in Eagle's Nest. It had satellite TV and heated floors. Dr. Leo Lacamoire had chosen it online, reading all the reviews and details and photos. He had picked Camp McCourt over Paul Bunyan's, across the lake, or Cubby Lodge, which had great breakfasts but no direct lake access. He had looked up the cabins on Google Earth, checking out at the views to find out from which he could best see the libr—

No! We aren't at that part of the story yet. I didn't know what Dr. Leo Lacamoire was looking at, not that night. I only knew that there was a man at Eagle's Nest who had seen me spying. I only knew my butt was fried if my mom found out. But I also knew that there was something about his face—that total and utter look of sadness and despair—that I had seen before.

I crept back up to the window as slowly as possible. Dr. Leo Lacamoire—then just a dude, one whose name I didn't know and thought I never would—was not looking at me anymore. He wasn't looking at the lake, either. He was staring at the sky.

"Mom?" I slunk into the office, which my grandparents had converted from a garage.

"What, hon?" She kept her eyes focused on the computer. "I thought you were going stargazing with Daddy."

"I am. I just wanted to know—um—who's staying in Eagle's Nest?"

"I don't know. You can look in the database. Why?"

"Just wondering. I spotted them moving in. He looked kinda familiar." I pulled out the spare laptop and brought up our guest-tracking software.

"Abigail," Mom said tiredly, "tell me you were not snooping through that telescope."

"Some accidental snooping may have occurred," I muttered, clicking on the Eagle's Nest file. Mom was the only one who called me Abigail. I hated it.

"We're going to get the cops called on us one of these days," Mom said, shaking her head. "Enough with the Peeping Thomasina act!"

"It was an *accident*! I knocked the telescope out of place." Scrolling . . . scrolling . . . finally. A name.

Dr. Leo Lacamoire. Paid in cash.

Dad popped his head in. He was wearing a backward baseball cap and holding two sweatshirts. "Ready, Abs?"

We took off toward Fishtrap Park, where we could set up our telescope without any cabin lights getting in the way. As we walked past Eagle's Nest, I glanced in the window, but the guy I now knew to be Dr. Leo Lacamoire wasn't there. Instead, there was a tall black woman pacing the porch. She was older than Blair, but not as old as my mom.

"Excuse me?" The woman stopped abruptly and bounded down the steps. "Are you the owner of this place?"

Dad smiled. "That would be me. Gary McCourt." He held out his hand and she shook it. My dad liked a firm handshake, and I could tell she delivered one.

"Simone Sinclair. We have an issue," she said, looking concerned.

"An issue?" asked Dad.

"There's a raccoon under the porch." She pointed. "We heard him all night scratching at the door, trying to get in."

"Hmm," said Dad slowly. "A *raccoon* issue."

"A big, fat, angry raccoon issue."

That's when I knew: Dr. Leo Lacamoire and Simone Sinclair? They weren't from Wisconsin. Mom and Dad always rolled their eyes at the tourists who came and were surprised at things like raccoons or coyotes.

"What do they want us to do, Gary?" Mom had asked a million times. "Go out with a slingshot and personally eliminate every mosquito in the northern hemisphere? You're in the *woods*. We have *bugs* here."

"I don't mean to cause, you know, a problem. It's just really keeping my boss up all night," said Simone. "And when he's up all night, he's not exactly a joy to be around. You know what I'm saying?"

"I do," said Dad seriously. "But the raccoon hasn't gotten *in*to the cabin?"

"Well, no. But its nest or something has to be under the porch."

"Den," said Dad.

"What?"

"Raccoons live in dens, not nests," he said. "But! Your point has been noted. I'll get someone over here first thing tomorrow morning to do a clean sweep."

"Thank you," she said, pressing her hands together.

"I really appreciate it. Seriously."

We kept walking, mostly in silence. I liked the nighttime lake noises—the loons calling and the waves lapping and the *thump*, *thump* of our footsteps. When we got to Fishtrap Park, my dad got the telescope on the stand while I tipped my head back and looked up.

If you want to catch stars, here's what you need to remember: you have to go somewhere dark. When I was a kid, we went on vacation to New York City. We couldn't see a single star in the sky because of all the lights. There's too much for them to compete with. You need to be in total darkness, where they're the only things worth looking at. And once you find the perfect stargazing spot, those stars go on for miles and miles, sparkling and winking and dotting the sky. It's like being in a whole new world when the stars are out, a world that doesn't have homework or mean girls or mosquito bites. I loved the stars, and the planets, and anything to do with the sky. Jade always said she could never see any of the constellations, but she just didn't know where to look. When she used to come along with Dad and me, her eyes were always on her phone, or down the road, as if waiting for something more interesting to pop out of nowhere. As if something could be more interesting than our very own galaxy.

"You ready?" asked Dad. "Three weeks."

I nodded. There was going to be a solar eclipse above North America, and little old Moose Junction had been named as *the* place to catch it at full totality. The moon would block the sun, and for a few minutes, it would be completely dark in the middle of the day. Our cabins had been booked for months, and there was going to be a huge viewing party on Main Street. The night of, *Star Wars: A New Hope* would be played on a huge projector to celebrate.

"Coontail's in town is already sold out of eclipse glasses, but hopefully they'll get another big shipment in," said Dad, adjusting the telescope height. "Safety first and all that."

"It's gonna be awesome," I said. Dad and I were the star people in our family. He taught astronomy during the school year at the community college three towns over. Mom and Jade usually thought the star maps scattered all over the attic were a bit much, but even they were stoked for the eclipse. Blair had been excited, too, before it all went to crap and she had to leave.

The telescope in the attic had been my twelfth birthday present last fall. I loved astronomy. It was basically just math in the sky. Everything could be measured or figured out or discovered with the right amount of time.

Because a person can have enough of passion, okay? Enough of art. A person can become tired of words like *fury* and *fate* and *destiny* and just want an answer. A person can want a world without big, wild, all-consuming feelings sometimes. Science was A + B = C, and maybe you didn't know what C was, but you knew you could figure it out. Blair had been a dancer. It was her *passion*, she had said a million times, convincing Mom she needed to drop out of school and take private lessons. But the way the music had swept her into a swirling mess of hopes and dreams? I never wanted to feel like that in my life. I'd seen how it chewed you up and spat you out. Passion was one of those things that seemed so beautiful from far away, until you got up close and it reached its hands out to grab you.

"It's really something, isn't it?" said Dad, peering at the moon. "Of all the places in the world, Moose Junction is the place to be this summer." Sure, we were known for our squeaky cheese curds and our musky competitions.

But it's not like people from the coasts were usually clamoring to spend their summer here.

Mom and Dad never told me much about business, but I knew that as more and more people wanted to go to places like Florida and Hawaii, fewer people were coming to the Northwoods. I didn't really get why—if you're going to be in the water, wouldn't you rather have a dock than sand? And be surrounded by trees instead of hotels? Sure, you can catch a glimpse of the constellations anywhere. But the total lack of real highways or skyscrapers made seeing them here something special. I also knew that this summer was going to be a huge boost for my parents. I'd heard Mom call the eclipse a gift from God while sorting through cabin deposits.

Jade could hate on where we lived—and she did—but from here, we could see the stars. That was what mattered to me.

"Come on, kiddo," said Dad. "I have a big meeting at City Hall in the morning." Dad was on the town selectman council for Moose Junction, and every month they had a meeting to decide on taxes and tourism and other boring stuff. I mean, I knew it was important—but I was also glad I didn't have to talk about any of it. As we walked back, we could see our breath with every exhale. Even in early August, the nights got so chilly around Moose Junction that you could find yourself wishing for some mittens. When we passed in front of Eagle's Nest, Simone was gone from the porch, and the house was completely dark.

"Gary! Abby!" Harrison waved from across the dirt road. He was one of our regulars; he came every August and stayed in Bluebird. "Stargazing? What a great night for it."

"Getting ready for the big eclipse," said Dad. "We can't wait."

"My two kids are coming that week. It's truly going to be something, isn't it? Hey, by the way, how's Blair doing? I heard about—well . . . I heard."

Blair McCourt. Eighteen years old, shiny brown hair, white teeth, sparkly eyes, ballerina, straight-A student, golden child. *Man, that girl's going places,* they used to say in town when she walked by. My sister and my best friend and my favorite person in the world.

Well, she sure went somewhere. Harvest Hills Center for Eating Disorders, where they could teach her how to eat again. Not exactly New York City.

Everyone was always asking about Blair in these sad

voices. Father Peter Patrick would grip Mom's hands after Mass and say he was praying for Blair. She always smiled and said thank you, but I could tell it made her feel weird. I mean, a whole town of people knowing your personal, private business is just strange, even when they're trying to be nice about it. It's like she was worried he was going to bring Blair up in a sermon or something.

Everybody needs their secrets. That's all I'm saying.

Dad just smiled. He was good in tense situations. Something about his eyes made everyone feel calmer. "She's doing well, Harrison. Thanks for asking. Hopefully coming home in the next few weeks here."

"Good. Good. You tell her to stay strong in there."

"Okay. We will. Good night now."

When we got home, I kissed Mom good night and headed to the attic. I had a hard time sleeping unless Jade was home, so I usually waited up for her with my eye through the telescope. I went to it, still pointed at Eagle's Nest, and looked through the window.

There he was, in the corner room, in the pitch-dark. Staring across the lake: Dr. Leo Lacamoire.

What's funny about the moon is that it's always the same size, even though we can only see slivers of it sometimes. It can be hard to see a full moon, glowing like a giant orb, and believe it's the same moon you can only see a tiny slice of on other nights. Right then, as I looked at Dr. Leo Lacamoire, I knew that I was only seeing a tiny slice. The world would turn, and the moon would orbit, and soon I'd see the whole thing. The reason Dr. Leo Lacamoire was in Moose Junction, Wisconsin, instead of at some resort in Tahiti or teaching astronauts at NASA. I would know the full story of the trials and tribulations of Dr. Leo Lacamoire, PhD, world-renowned scientist. But right then, that sad, sad sliver of a face was all I could see.

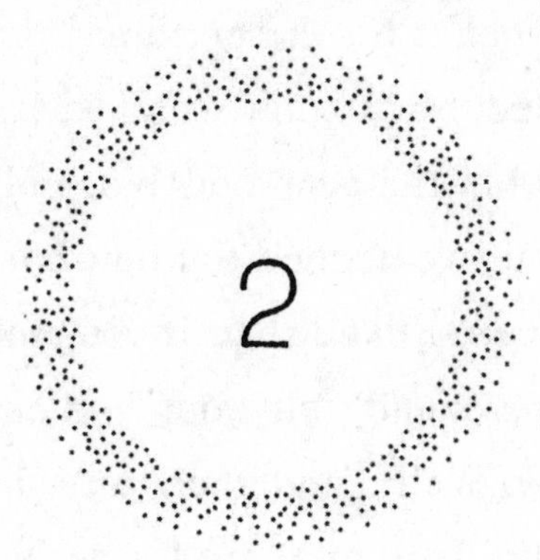

For the story to make sense, you will need to know about Blair. Telling my own story without telling Blair's would be like looking at the stars without a telescope. Sure, you can catch a glimpse, but you're not getting the full story.

Everyone knows about Blair, it feels like. She's been the main character of every chapter of my life. But I don't remember how we got from *then* to *now*, to be honest. I wish I could pinpoint a day where everything went wrong and circle it in red and drape it with yellow *Caution* tape. But it wasn't a day; it was a long, drawn-out fall that crashed when it hit the bottom. I don't even know when we slipped, I just know when we landed.

For our end-of-the-year oral biography report, Mr. Linn had told us we needed to know our subjects *backward and forward.* I liked that. If you really understood something, you could tell your audience what happened chronologically, and then turn around and tell it in reverse. I'd done mine on Katherine Johnson, the woman who helped calculate the trajectory of space launches for NASA. We wouldn't have been able to send John Glenn up to the stars without her and her brain. Four other girls in class had done Amelia Earhart, and Marissa Mulligan had even worn a real leather pilot's jacket. But nobody in our class had even known who Katherine Johnson was, except for a few kids who had seen some big movie about her, and I could tell you everything you needed to know about her, from the day she was born to where she lived today and vice versa. I got an A.

So maybe to fully understand the story of Blair, I should tell it backward.

Maybe then, you can see what we all missed.

THIS PAST MAY

Twelve years old

Exactly ten weeks before I spotted Dr. Leo Lacamoire in the window that night, our town held the Moose Junction Memorial Day Bash. As Leo poured over Google images of Moose Junction, finding the best resort to stay at, looking at pictures of the Moose Junction Public Library from every angle he could find, I pulled on a red-and-white tank top and loaded up on the bug spray. It was the beginning of summer, and you could feel it in the air, the way the sun found our pale shoulders and the turtles had returned to their log on Fishtrap Lake. The eclipse seemed ages away, an end-of-summer treat, a reward for making it through tourist season.

By Memorial Day, the tourists had arrived in full force and Main Street was packed. The Bash was our annual kickoff to summer, the biggest block party we had all year. The Cranberry Patch Gift Shop had a line out the door of people looking for real maple syrup and Lou's cranberry coffee blend. Northern Lights had just bought an espresso machine so you could get more than a lukewarm cup of blah, and Hank's Hardware and More had a sale on buoys and coolers. Music was blaring; I saw Caleb Evers playing drums and waved. He gave me a nod.

Most years, I went to the party with Sophie and Lex from school. Moose Junction was so small that the three of us had to ride the bus for forty-five minutes every morning to get to Waukegan County Middle and those forty-five minutes got pretty long if you didn't like who you were with. Thankfully, we did.

"Abby," Sophie said suddenly, as we stood outside Coontail's with our newly purchased bottled waters, "is that—um, is that Blair?"

After what had happened in the spring with her Joffrey audition, Blair had gone from Golden Girl to Ghost. She spent most of her time in her bedroom or at the ballet studio in Milwaukee. And following the prom fiasco, Mom had taken Blair's car away and was driving her herself. It was a two-hour commute; I barely saw either of them.

I had asked Blair that morning if she wanted to just skip the Memorial Day party all together.

"We could do the paddleboards?" I asked her, standing in her doorway. "Or just hang out on the dock . . ."

"Maybe," she said. She was digging around in a bag of pointe shoes, trying to find a pair that wasn't completely destroyed. She could go through a pair of them in a week, easy. My tank top seemed too cheerful and summery in her room; she was dressed in a thick gray Camp McCourt sweatshirt and a pair of jeans. She even had fuzzy gray socks on, covering her ripped-up feet.

Mom popped her head in. "You girls should go to the party. It will be fun," she said, trying to sound cheerful. I think she just wanted something to stay the same: after a year where it seemed as if all our plans and routines and order had flown out the window, this one thing, this one day, could stay the same as it always was. I didn't blame her. But I also didn't blame Blair, who was going to be the center of attention. She was *always* the center of attention, but it used to be because she was so talented. Now it was because everyone had heard about Joffrey and was doing that awkward don't-ask-about-it shuffle around her.

I shrugged. "It was just an idea. If you want to go to the party, go to the party."

Blair sighed, grabbing some jet glue and dabbing it on a slip of fabric that had been worn off the toe. "Yeah, I think I'll go to Main Street. Whatever. I don't even know where my swimsuit is."

That's because you refuse to wear anything that shows your skin, I wanted to scream. We all stood there awkwardly for a beat before Mom went back to the laundry and I pulled out my phone to text Sophie.

So there we were: at the party. All Blair's shininess was gone. She was hollow, like an emptied-out tree in the dead of winter. She and I had the same brown hair—Jade got Mom's blond genes—and while hers used to look thick and beautiful in a French twist with a spotlight on it, it was now so thin that a million bobby pins couldn't hold it in place. She had kept her sweatshirt on, too, looking completely out of place at a beginning-of-summer party. Our family was pretty pale by nature, and it *was* spring in Wisconsin, but the skin on her face was nearly see-through. Ghost Girl. Like I said. I felt as if she could take a single step and crack into a thousand pieces, turning into Blair dust and floating around the street.

She was talking to Joe from the hardware store. *What are your plans for next year?* That stupid question, over and over and over again, reminding us all that the answer was a big fat question mark—and *not* the Joffrey. Or college. Or much of anything.

Blair just kind of shrugged, looking bored. "Not sure yet. I have a ballet competition this summer . . ."

"I heard about that," said Joe. "I'm sure you'll do great." I wished some of his hopefulness would wear off on the rest of us.

"We'll see," said Blair.

"You'll figure it out," replied Joe, patting her shoulder. "Don't you worry."

She flinched when his hand met her shoulder.

"I'm not worried." But her voice was high and tight, as if she was trying not to cry.

A girl from her old high school walked by, too. Jessica-Now-Jess, Blair called her, since she'd decided to reinvent herself by dropping the second half of her name and dyeing her hair blue. Like you could make a town the size of ours think you were a whole new person with a box of dye from Coontail's and a new nickname. The two of them had been . . . lab partners? English project partners? *Something* or other, before Blair had opted for homeschool so she could focus on ballet.

"Blair. Omigod, it's been *forever*." Jessica-Now-Jess threw her arms around my sister as if they were the best of friends. Blair didn't look happy about it.

"Hey."

"Hey. I heard about Julliard—"

"Joffrey," Blair corrected her with a tight smile.

"Yeah. That tryout for the ballet school? That's so awful."

Lex whispered something to Sophie, and my face got hot.

"Yeah, that's her," I finally answered Sophie, looking away. "Come on." I tried to pull my friends forward.

"Wait, I needed sunscreen," said Sophie. "Sorry. I'm so flipping pale right now, I'll be like a tomato in an hour. Curse of the redhead. Don't leave without me." She ducked back inside, leaving Lex and me to watch the train wreck unfold.

Jessica-Now-Jess was going on about how she was so sorry about the Joffrey Incident. She reached over and grabbed her elbow, which Blair yanked back.

"You don't need this sweatshirt. Omigod. It's a million degrees out here." She giggled. "All that time in dance practice? You could probably use some sun."

"I'm cold," said Blair, getting agitated. I wanted to step in and whisk her away from this obnoxious girl. We'd all gotten good at managing Blair; avoiding certain topics and not commenting on her bizarre fashion choices. There were meanings under meanings, reasons under reasons, a sweatshirt hiding sharp elbows and keeping warm a girl whose body couldn't even regulate its own temperature. Jessica-Now-Jess needed to move along.

"Whatever you say," she said, fanning herself dramatically.

Thankfully, right as Lex glanced back into the store to see if Sophie had finished paying for her Banana Boat, Jessica-Now-Jess turned to leave, waving goodbye and shouting "I'll text you," which, hopefully, she wouldn't. Blair looked like she'd rather be anywhere else. She should have just stayed home.

Sophie emerged, holding a bottle of sunscreen. Finally. I crossed the street with the two of them to get closer to the music. Then I heard the commotion.

"Just try it, girl. Good God, you're skin and bones." It was Miss Mae. She was shoving a chocolate fudge cupcake under Blair's nose. Miss Mae sat in the front row of Mass every Sunday and rolled her eyes at half the things Father Peter Patrick said. She was always going off about communists. I wasn't even sure what a communist was, but Miss Mae could convince you your own neighbor was one. She'd utter it like you would the words *serial killer*.

But at that moment, she wasn't worried about the communists.

"I'm okay," Blair was saying, pushing the cupcake away. "I'm—"

"Listen, child, you are *too skinny*. Just a taste. You only live once. I mean, how can you even dance with those skeleton legs?"

"I have a dairy allergy," said Blair icily. "So thanks, but no thanks."

I held my breath. It was too much, all of it. The questions without answers, the Joffrey mention, the missing swimsuit, and now a cupcake, Miss Mae's thumb leaving a fingerprint in the frosting.

"It's delicious. One small bite." Miss Mae was *loud*. Too loud. Her voice was like a speaker with the volume turned up full blast. People were staring. My heart was thumping in my chest. *Stop it*, I begged her. *Stop it stop it sto—*

"I said *no thank you!*" Blair shrieked. It was so intense the music stopped playing. Everyone was looking now, a sea of eyes—some we knew but most from Chicago or Madison or Milwaukee, here to swim in the lakes and grill hot dogs. Not to see a Ghost Girl lose it.

It was Jessica-Now-Jess and Joe and a swimsuit versus a sweatshirt. The reasons under reasons had cracked to the core, revealing the truest reason: my sister was Not Okay.

I ripped away from Sophie and Lex, but I wasn't fast enough. Blair was screaming, thrashing, crying, and my mother's arms were wrapped around her, and that was how the world ended: over a stupid half-melted cupcake.

"Blair is going away for the summer," Mom said.

Mom, Jade, and I were sitting around the dinner table. It was a Family Meeting without two very important family members. Our dog, Obi, snuggled up against my feet. He was a Norwegian elkhound, bred to be a guardian and defender. He could sense our tension like most dogs could sense a squirrel. He was huge, but like Dad said, if you're going to get a dog, go big or go home.

"Where's she going?" I asked.

"A place that can help her get better," Mom said gently.

"Like a hospital?" Jade chewed on the end of her ponytail. The purple streak was new, but Mom and Dad hadn't said a word. Jade could do anything she wanted. I could paint one of my fingernails purple and probably be thrown in prison. I don't know why; that's just the way it went. I learned sooner rather than later that when your siblings are messed up, you have to be the steady one. The last thing Mom needed was another daughter with Issues.

"Sort of. It's like . . . a therapy center. A place where she can get the treatment she needs, and doctors, and people to make her food . . . help her eat. It's in Madison."

"How long does she have to go for?" I asked. "What about ballet?"

Blair was a ballerina. She wasn't just good; she was amazing. She'd been homeschooled for the past two years so that she could spend more time training at her studio in Milwaukee. I loved watching her dance. Jade did, too, I could tell. Even though she usually said it was lame and brought her iPhone and earbuds. I looked over at her screen once, though, and nothing was playing. She was just being a brat.

"Initially, six weeks, then we'll check in," Mom said. "Maybe twelve. I'm not sure. And ballet isn't important right now."

But ballet was the *only* thing that was important to Blair. It was her entire life. It was her future, she'd told me a million times, stretching her feet and pulling them above her head, toes reaching toward the ceiling. It was her destiny.

"Yeah, right," snorted Jade. "Tell the Sugar Plum Fairy that."

"Shut up," I said. This was an old dance, me and Blair versus Jade. Three sisters, but we were unbalanced. Blair and I liked Star Wars and had brown hair and liked hanging out. Jade was ice blond, wanted nothing to do with us, and thought we read too much. And now I was losing my teammate, even though it hadn't felt like we were on the same team for a while.

"Girls. Please. I have enough of a headache as it is," Mom said, rubbing her temple. "Blair's upstairs packing. Make sure you say goodbye to her tonight. We're leaving in the morning. Jade, I need you in the office tomorrow, and please don't argue with me."

She'd already begun to open her mouth, but closed it.

"Where's Dad?" I asked.

"On the phone with the insurance company," Mom muttered, looking like her headache had just gotten ten times worse.

"One more question," said Jade, laying her hands flat on the table. "Does Blair *want* to go? Or are you making her go?"

"A little of both," she responded. "Sometimes that's a mom's job. To make decisions for you that are for the best even when you disagree. But Blair knows she's sick. And she does want to get better."

All we could do was nod.

Mom had to find some numbers for Dad, so I went upstairs and knocked on Blair's door. Obi trotted after me, ready to snuggle away any tension.

"What."

I pushed the door open. I'd always been jealous of Blair with her own room. All I wanted was to decorate mine the way *I* wanted, without Jade's freaky rock band posters or dirty jeans on the floor. Blair's room was painted a pretty mint color, and her furniture was all shiny white. She had a trunk that was filled to the brim with turn boards to help her perfect her pirouettes, and a poster of Misty Copeland tacked to the wall beside it. Her huge bag of beat-up pointe shoes was shoved in the corner, but besides that, the room was immaculate.

"Mom said you're leaving," I whispered tentatively. This was Blair, my best friend, my fearless leader. I would have walked across burning coals for her a thousand times over. Now she felt like a stranger.

"Yup," she said flatly, shoving a bathrobe into a suitcase without folding it. Obi circled the room, sniffing out danger.

"Well," I continued, "I thought maybe you'd want to take this." I held our notebook out to her. It was a black-and-white composition notebook, the kind kids in the 1950s had to take to school before we all got iPads.

It was filled with pages and pages of our finest creation:

Planet Pirates. It was a comic we'd come up with that had everything we loved: space and princesses and even ballet sometimes. Blair and I loved Star Wars—hence why our dog's full name was Obi-Wan Kenobi McCourt—and we were convinced we could make something just as epic and become millionaires. She sketched first, and I wrote the stories to go with her pictures. Blair was an even better artist than she was a ballerina, but she didn't think so.

For years we'd been working on *Planet Pirates*. We'd sent Captain Antoine Moonbeard on adventures to Mars and the moon and the Milky Way to save Princess Stardust. Not even Jade was allowed to touch the notebook. This was our thing, the thing that connected us through food being pushed around plates and bloodied-toe tights being pulled off too-thin legs. We'd spent less and less time on our comic over the past few months, but it was still there, waiting to be filled with our stories.

"It's your turn," I said lamely. "I thought you'd want to see what I wrote for your last few drawings. I know we haven't worked on it in a while, but . . ."

She stared at the notebook, and then at me. I thought maybe she would yell or tell me to get Obi out; he was shedding all over her comforter. But instead, she put her head in her hands and started to cry.

Blair the bold, Blair the strong, Blair the tough. People thought ballet dancers were flimsy little fairies, but Blair had punched Isaac Frank in the nose when he called her a sissy in fourth grade. She could perform onstage in front of hundreds of people and not even feel nervous. Yet here she was, crumbling to pieces in front of me.

That wasn't the Blair I knew. I couldn't even look. It was like staring into the eclipse without glasses. Your eyes could burn off.

I ran out into the hallway. When I reached my room, I slammed my door shut and locked it, even though that wasn't allowed. *Our family doesn't lock our doors*, Mom had reminded us a thousand times.

Blair hadn't needed to lock a door, though, to keep this secret.

I turned my fan on full blast and pulled a blanket over my head, squeezing my eyes closed.

The night went on but I stayed in my room, unlocking the door only for Jade, who came in and went to sleep without saying a word. The next morning, Mom called for us to come down and say goodbye. I ignored her. When she came up and poked her head in our room, I pretended to be asleep.

"It's fine, Mom. I said goodbye to her yesterday," Blair said.

I heard the car doors open and shut a few times. Then Dad's truck started and pulled out of the driveway, crunching over gravel. Just like that, she was gone.

I stayed there, under my covers, willing everything to go back to how it had been.

But it wouldn't. Blair got diagnosed with anorexia, which sounded like a person to me: Anna Rexia, an evil witch who hides under your bed and sets your hair on fire. If I had Blair's artistic talent, I would have drawn her—a super-skinny woman, almost see-through yet covered with fur, with red eyes and spiky hair. Anna Rexia tricked the scale and whispered lies into your ears and pointed out how many calories things were. She tripped you in ballet class and poured salt into your eyes so that you couldn't see what was real and what wasn't. Anna Rexia had found my sister and taken her hostage. Even when Blair left, Anna was there—hiding behind curtains, humming softly. If you stopped to listen, you could hear her.

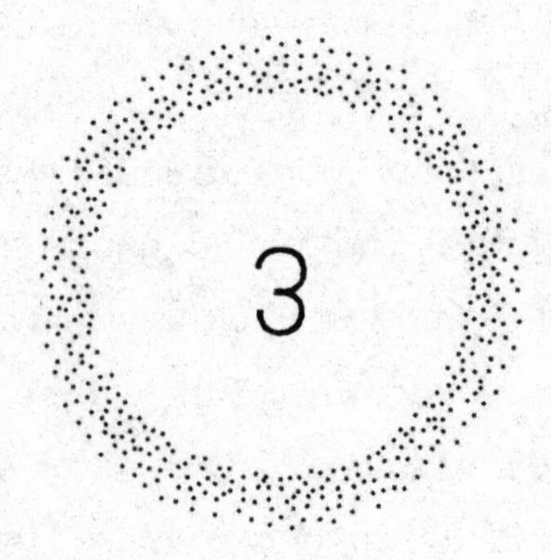

AUGUST, PRESENT DAY

Twelve years old

The morning after spying on Dr. Leo Lacamoire, I was woken up by Obi.

"Ugh. Kibble breath." I hauled him up onto my comforter and snuggled him tight, but he wiggled out of my grip. Obi wanted your love and affection right up until the moment you gave it to him.

"Abigail?" Mom called. "Up and at 'em. I have to run into town, so you need to be in the office."

"Child labor laws are a thing, you know," I yelled back.

"Do you have anything better to do?" she asked.

Low blow. But point taken.

I got out of bed and yanked on some shorts and a tank top before quickly brushing my teeth. As I did, I stared at myself in the bathroom mirror. Tall, white, brown hair, medium weight: a handful of traits that didn't really say much about me. Blair thought she was fat, even though she obviously wasn't—she didn't even weigh a hundred pounds. Did that mean she thought *I* was fat? I had asked Mom that one time, and she quickly shook her head, saying that wasn't how eating disorders worked. It was more about control than judging other people. It had never crossed my mind before, except when Sophie and I went swimsuit shopping and sucked in our stomachs in the mirror. I was a normal weight for my height, which was too tall already and kept creeping up when I wasn't looking. I was probably skinnier than half the girls at school and fatter than the other half.

But I couldn't stop thinking about what Blair would think of how *I* looked.

Obi followed behind like a shadow. We left the house and jogged over to the office.

"We should really get an air conditioner in here," I grumbled, grabbing a bottle of water from the fridge.

"Thanks, honey," Mom said, grabbing a notepad off the office table with a list of things she needed in town. "I have to go get some light bulbs for Maple Leaf. You're on the phone, okay?"

"Got it," I said.

Just as she took off, Jade ducked in.

"Hey," she said. "Dad went on a run. He told me to tell you he'd relieve you after three miles. I'm about to go floating with some friends, so I'll see you later." During the summer in Moose Junction, everyone loved tying pool floats together and floating down Musky River. Jade and her crew would bring a huge cooler of soda and stay out there all day. Blair would take me sometimes, before she stopped really doing anything fun. I almost felt like calling Sophie and Lex to see about getting together later, but I hadn't seen them hardly at all since Memorial Day. I'd bumped into Sophie at Coontail's and we'd talked for a few minutes, but she didn't ask me to go swimming or anything. I guess I didn't ask *her*, either, but it felt like they were avoiding me. A couple of weeks ago I had asked them to come over, but Lex wasn't feeling well and Sophie was going to see her cousins. Neither of them had texted me the next day to see if I still wanted to hang out. After Mom had mentioned seeing them at the Ice Shanty getting ice cream, I triple-checked my phone to be sure I hadn't missed any texts.

I hadn't.

But summer was almost over. Soon, we'd all be back on that school bus for one last year at Waukegan Middle. I'd spent most of my summer helping out in the office and reading fantasy books. While everyone else in town was on vacation, here to have Big Summer Adventures, I was answering phones and reminding Mom about the broken dishwasher in Robin's Egg. It left me with a lot of time to think about things I didn't want to think about, Blair and my friends topping that list.

"Excuse me?" a voice called. "Anybody here?"

Jade and I glanced up. Standing there was Simone—looking less than pleased.

"Um, hi," I said. "Can I help you?"

She raised an eyebrow. "Isn't there anybody a little older around here?"

"My mom's in town," I explained. "But do you need new pillowcases or something? I know where everything is."

She sighed. "There's a hole in our door now."

"A *what*?" I asked.

"A hole . . . Chewed by some sort of animal or something," she said.

"The raccoon," I said meekly.

"The raccoon," she confirmed. "He needs to be dealt with ASAP. The thing kept me up all night. And now there's a gaping hole in our door, and mosquitos are coming through. Not to mention that anybody who walks by can see right in . . ."

"I'm sorry about that," I said. "As soon as my dad gets here, I can send him over to fix the door. And handle the raccoon."

"Thank you," she said with a sigh, picking up a brochure for a fishing supply store and fanning herself. "I don't mean to cause a ruckus here. But my boss is driving me nuts."

"Understandable," I assured her.

"He's just so . . ." She threw her hands in the air. "Well. Anyway. Not your problem. Listen: this seems like a pretty good gig. Stick with it and *never* accept a job as an assistant for a scientist, no matter how brilliant. Hear me?"

"Heard," I said with a smile.

"I'll be at the cabin. Tell your dad to please, please

come as fast as he can. My boss likes his privacy, and a big old hole in the door isn't providing it." She turned and left.

"It's just a racoon," muttered Jade.

I shrugged. "It did chew a hole in her door. In the most expensive cabin. And it sounds like she didn't sleep all night."

Jade rolled her eyes. "Whatever. I'm out of here." She grabbed a few waters from the fridge and took off.

Jade and I had never really been buddies; she'd had her own friends. Blair had never been Miss Popular since she was always at dance and couldn't go to normal things like sleepovers, but she still invited me to the stuff she did go to. If I showed up somewhere Jade and her friends were, Jade would have a heart attack. She basically wanted me to disappear. That was fine with me. Her and her friends didn't talk about anything more important than lip gloss and listened to screechy music. It's not like they wanted to learn about Katherine Johnson or how to find Scorpius.

I bummed around in the office, scrolling through Sophie's Instagram feed. I was right; they were totally avoiding me. There was picture after picture of her and Lex—floating on Musky River, paddleboarding, giving kissy faces in front of the fireworks on the Fourth of July. They even got together with some other kids from school and went to a Brewers game in Milwaukee. Whatever. I pulled up our group text, which had been full of jokes and homework questions and invitations to hang out during the school year. Now it had dwindled to practically nothing.

I clicked over to Caleb Evers's feed. He didn't have as many pictures, but there were still a few of him and his friends gathered around a dock. A couple of him holding a big fish. I looked back even further, to spring.

There was the picture from prom. Blair, smiling in her shiny pink dress that we'd all gone shopping for together. Caleb had his hand on her back, and he was looking right at her.

"Abby?" I slammed the laptop shut as my dad walked in behind me. "Whoa, state secrets or something?"

"Nothing," I muttered.

"I'm here to let you off the hook," said Dad, wiping the sweat off his forehead. "Man, it's hot out there. Why don't you go jump in the lake? Call the girls or something."

I shrugged. They had my phone number. If they had wanted to hang out with me this summer, they could have.

"Simone came by," I said. "From Eagle's Nest? That

raccoon chewed a hole through the door."

"Oh man. You gotta be kidding me." He groaned. "I'll go fix it. I need to call Mom and have her pick up some extra plywood first. I hope she's still in town. Can you run down there and tell them I'll be there as soon as Mom gets back?"

Go to Eagle's Nest?

And *talk* to Dr. Leo Lacamoire?

My heart jumped.

There was something about our newest resort guest that seemed big. *Momentous*, Mr. Linn would have said, like John Glenn orbiting the Earth for the first time. Some shift happening in the summer that I couldn't quite place my finger on. Dr. Leo Lacamoire was not an ordinary visitor, and even though I didn't know it just yet, I knew that it was going to be . . . significant. Sort of like when you see somebody at the airport or the mall and you can't stop staring at them even though you're not sure why. That was how I felt about him.

I know, I know. A + B = C. Sure. But passion, adventure—you can *say* you don't want those things. You can watch them destroy a person and ruin a summer. That doesn't mean they don't hide under your bed sometimes, waiting for you to notice them.

"I'll go right now," I said.

I walked over to Eagle's Nest and knocked carefully on the front door. I could hear music coming from inside, but not the type of music that bugs Dad—loud rap or country played at full volume that messes with the peace of the woods—but classical, like the kind Blair would dance to.

The hole in the door wasn't so big, but raccoons can stuff themselves through spaces smaller than you'd think.

"Hello?" I called out tentatively.

I don't know what made me step inside, but I did. I had been in all our cabins a million times, but Eagle's Nest was by far our nicest. It looked barely lived in, though, besides the cereal box on the counter and the slightly messed-up blanket folded on the couch. It was less of a "cabin" and more of a rustic-chic house that was way nicer than ours. It had a huge spiral staircase in the middle of the first floor leading up to the lookout, a round room with huge windows. It was where I had seen Dr. Leo Lacamoire the night before, peering out onto the lake.

"*Hello?*" I called out again. Nobody answered, but I could hear the classical music. It was coming from above me.

I took the stairs slowly, realizing that this wasn't just any classical music. This was something Blair *had* danced to at a recital once. I remembered it because, at the end, she had some super tricky turn that she'd practiced over and over. That music was practically tattooed onto my brain. The farther I climbed up the steps, the noisier it got. Violins, trumpets, and piano cascaded across the house in a swirl of sound that made me think of guys in poofy wigs. It gave me goose bumps. Loud, clashing, and dramatic. *Passion. Destiny.* The sort of sound that sped up your heart.

I pushed open the door at the top. There he was, not through a telescope but standing five feet away from me: Dr. Leo Lacamoire, glasses low on his nose, looking intensely at something on his desk.

For a second, I just stared. Every inch of him was concentrating, from his shoulder blades to his knees. It was like he was trying to will a star into existence.

"Excuse me?" I said. The music was turned up so high you wouldn't have heard Obi howl, let alone me.

"*Excuse me?*" I yelled. He jumped a foot in the air when he saw me, and screamed like a little kid. Which made me scream, too.

"Who are you? What are you doing up here?" he

exclaimed over the music in a thick British accent.

"The raccoon," I shouted.

"What?" he shouted back. I pointed to the speakers. He rolled his eyes dramatically before reaching over and turning the music down. He was going to have hearing loss one day if he kept his music that ear-piercing all the time. I was surprised a raccoon was brave enough to come in.

"The *raccoon*," I said. "I'm Abby McCourt. My dad is the resort manager. He sent me here to tell you that he'll be over really soon to fix the hole."

"The hole?" He looked confused. Was this guy older than I thought? Maybe he had some kind of a memory issue. Before our grandma died, she used to call all three of us Julie, like my mom, or Elizabeth, who was some friend of hers growing up. She once showed up at the grocery store without her shoes on.

"In your door," I said. "Simone came to the office and said you needed it fixed pronto." *Pronto?* Why did I say that? It made me sound like a cowboy in an old movie. Nobody said words like *pronto* in real life. Something about Dr. Leo Lacamoire could make a person very nervous.

"Simone," he said. "Yes, right. She's in town. I told her I needed some room to breathe. I'm working, so, if you don't mind . . ." He waved a hand across his desk as if to show me how busy he was. There were messy stacks of paper, and—

Telescopes.

Multiple telescopes. Fancy kinds that you'd see in a museum, all set up by the large window. And those weren't just pieces of paper, they were star charts.

"You like stars?" I asked, surprised.

He looked at me like Jade looked at Obi when he burst into the bathroom as she got ready. Like, *Out of my personal space, please.* "Yes," he said shortly.

I stood there awkwardly, a million thoughts circling my mind. Could I look through one of those telescopes? Was he a professional, or just one of those super serious nerds who went to conventions and stuff? Was he here for the eclipse? I didn't want this to be my only interaction with Dr. Leo Lacamoire, apparent astronomer.

But he kept glancing at me, clearly annoyed, so I turned to go.

"Wait," he barked. "I have a question."

I turned back. "Yeah?"

"The library," he said. "Do you know its hours? Nothing in this godforsaken town has a website."

"Eight to eight, Monday through Saturday. Closed on

Sundays," I told him. I wasn't just a fountain of helpful Moose Junction facts. I also loved the library. It was one of those safe, sacred spaces where I could run away to Narnia or Middle-earth or Hogwarts, curled up in one of its cozy beanbags, pretending Blair knew how to eat and my friends were still my friends and Jade didn't hate me. The librarian, Harriet, was one of my favorite people in the universe. The fact that Dr. Leo Lacamoire might be a library person, though, I hadn't seen coming. We were kind of a dying breed, in the age of Google and tablets and free shipping. Not many people wanted to flip through a paperback that had someone else's hot chocolate stains on chapter four.

"Thanks," he said shortly, turning back to his maps.

"I'll . . . I'll tell Dad not to bother you when he gets here," I said. "Just to fix the hole."

Dr. Leo Lacamoire nodded, not even looking up.

I bounded back down the stairs and out the door, letting it bang closed behind me. Dad was sitting in the office, typing on a calculator.

"I told him," I said. "He's working upstairs, though. Said not to bug him. Just fix the hole."

"Got it," said Dad. "I caught your mom just before she left the hardware store, luckily."

"What are you doing?" I asked, pointing toward the calculator.

"Oh, just moving some numbers around," sighed Dad. "That meeting last night was . . . well, there's not enough money in the world, Abby. That's all there is to it."

I shook my head. "Taylor Swift? Hello, Dad. Some people can fly to Paris to get dessert just because they feel like it."

"I think that was Kim What's-Her-Face," Dad said.

"Kardashian. You know her name," I said. Dad liked to pretend he didn't read the gossipy tabloids Jade left in the office, even though he clearly did.

"Well, fine. Sure. But think of the kids in parts of the world who don't even know where dinner is coming from. Kids in *Milwaukee*, even. Kids down the road. Money can be hard to find," Dad said. "And our town doesn't have enough of it. Everything's taking a hit. If you guys want art classes next year, if you want the library to stay open—"

"*What?*" The library couldn't close. The thought of living in a town without a library made my skin crawl.

"This eclipse better be everything they say," Dad said. "We're booked to capacity. So are Paul Bunyan's and Cubby Lodge. Even the Blue Moon Motel." We both shivered. Let's just say when you drove past the Blue Moon Motel, you wondered who would ever stay there. The owner, Harvey, wore those creepy white tank tops all the time, even in November.

"The economy could use a boost. At least a high five," Dad said. "That's all."

I crossed my fingers. "Here's hoping."

"Wish upon one of your stars or something," Dad said. "Hey, we're going to see Blair tomorrow . . . are you coming?"

I shook my head. My ponytail whipped my cheeks.

"Abby . . ."

I'm terrible at team sports. I scraped by with a C in art last year because my shooting star sculpture looked more like a rock. Mrs. Schroeder winced in choir when I tried out for a solo, even though she tried to deny it. My skills are *limited*, okay? If it doesn't involve a telescope or a comic book, I'm hopeless. But one thing I *am* very good at: avoidance. I could gold medal in it. I hurried out of the office, leaving Dad and his calculator and his mention of my sister behind me like dust.

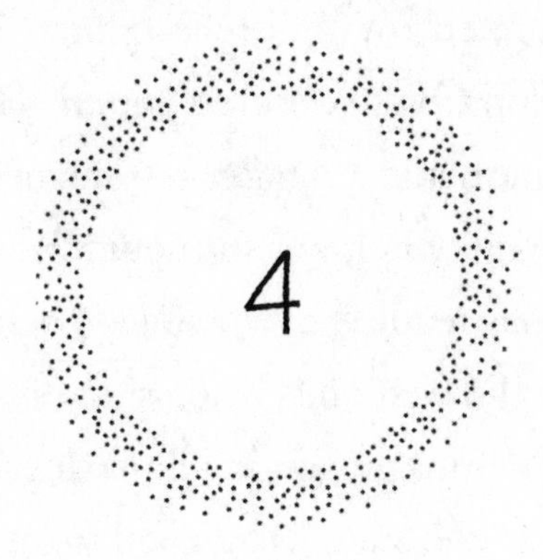

AUGUST, PRESENT DAY

Twelve years old

The next day, the clouds rolled in. When it storms in the Northwoods, the rain waits and waits and waits before dropping a downpour on you that lasts for what seems like ages. I felt bad for the tourists who came with swimsuits and fishing poles. But I didn't mind when it rained in the summer. It was kind of a nice break from feeling like you had to constantly be doing something fun and outdoorsy. Like, I live on a resort. Most people's vacation is just my *life.* And sometimes it gets tiring.

So when it rains, I usually head to the library.

"Hey, Harriet," I said, ducking in out of the crazy

weather. I dropped my umbrella behind her desk. She barely looked up from a tattered paperback. Harriet was black, supersmart, and . . . bigger. Some of the other kids in town made fun of her, but she couldn't have cared less. She was too busy reading every single book in the library and giving me the best ones when she was done. She was probably my favorite person in all of Moose Junction.

"Hey, Abby," she said. "You good today?"

"I'm good," I assured her. If you didn't know what you wanted to read, Harriet could find it. She was the master at getting books in the hands of people who'd love them. Even Sophie, who didn't like anything without a vampire. She was a lot better than Josiah, the college kid who helped out in the summer and pushed old history books on anyone who walked through the door. You'd come in looking for a cozy mystery and leave with *The Life and Times of John Adams, Extended Edition*.

I didn't usually need a lot of help, though. I was pretty much a Professional Library Browser. I knew all the tricks, like getting on your knees to see what was on the bottom shelf—the best stuff always got ignored down there—and giving a book the tried and true two-paragraph test.

But today I was off my game. Nothing seemed to stand out. I stuck my head back around to the desk.

"Hey, Harriet? Did you get the new Star Wars book?"

"No," she said. "I could only get ten new books this summer and it didn't make the cut."

I groaned. "Are you kidding? *Ten?*"

"You're telling me," said Harriet, rolling her eyes. "Every year it's less and less. This town. I swear."

"My dad mentioned something about it," I said. "That we aren't swimming in dough."

"Treading water is more like it," said Harriet. "We had to send Josiah back to Madison and everything."

"Seriously?"

Harriet swooped her arm across the empty library. "It isn't exactly bustling in here, Abby. They thought we didn't need two librarians."

I suddenly missed Josiah. I almost had an urge to go pick up *Abraham Lincoln: A History of America's Greatest Leader*.

Instead, I found a fantasy book I'd read a million times and curled up in my favorite beanbag chair by the huge window. Thunderstorm outside, just me and Harriet inside, and a book about a princess, a quest, and spaceships—*yeah*. It felt right, that instant *click* you get when you're doing exactly what you want to be doing. There were no money problems in this particular galaxy.

Whenever I read fantasy, I made sure not to let it influence *Planet Pirates* too much. It might seem stupid, fine, but I was still holding on to some kind of weird hope that one day we'd get discovered and *Planet Pirates* would be huge. We'd make it big, me and Blair, and we could tour the country. Our stories, of Captain Moonbeard and Princess Stardust, would be read by millions of people and they'd make movies out of them, like Star Wars, where people would wait in line at midnight. So I didn't want to accidentally plagiarize, or even make things too similar. I was trying to be original.

I had shown Sophie some of our drawings once and she had gotten all excited, saying we needed to mail them off to a fancy publisher. I couldn't help it—I had started daydreaming. Spending most of my life writing alongside Blair sounded like a pretty good plan. So, sure, sometimes I thought about what it would be like to slide our creation into an envelope and mail it to New York. To get a phone call saying we were going to be famous authors and Marvel wanted to make *Planet Pirates* into a movie.

It was dumb. I knew that. But you can't help your head from dreaming. Wishes aren't a faucet you can just turn off.

Anyway, we'd probably never work on *Planet Pirates* again. Blair couldn't draw when her hands were so shaky.

I stayed in the library for a while—one hour, two hours, three hours—until Mom texted me that they were on their way back from visiting Blair and that she wanted me home when they got there. I checked out the book and a few others, waving goodbye to Harriet as I left.

When Mom and Dad arrived, I could tell that there'd been an Issue. My mom's ponytail was all frazzled and my dad's jaw was clenched. Jade had to leave for the movie theater. Dad went to check how the new door at Eagle's Nest was holding up and Mom practically fell onto the couch.

"We need food," said Mom. "Pizza or Chinese?"

"Pizza," I said. *How's Blair?* It was on the tip of my tongue, but I couldn't ask it. I wanted to pretend they'd been somewhere else all day. Or maybe visiting Blair at the Joffrey, not Harvest Hills.

She pulled out her phone to order pizza from the delivery app. "What did you do today?"

"Nothing. Library." *How's Blair? How's Blair? How's Blair?*

"Pepperoni or sausage? Both?"

"Whatever, Mom. I don't care," I snapped.

"Geez, Abby, cut me some slack. I'm just trying to feed you here. I had a long, crappy day. Go easy on me."

"Sorry," I muttered.

Mom typed for a minute more, then set the phone down and put a hand over her eyes. We sat in silence.

"We're trying to figure out a transition plan," she said. "For when Blair comes home. What she'll *do* all year. She was supposed to be at—well, college. Or something." She was *supposed* to be at the Joffrey. We had all thought so. We thought we'd be picking out hotels in New York City, not figuring out transition plans.

"Is she going to live here?"

"Of course," said Mom. "Of *course.* This is her *home.* But there are so many things to be considered. Therapy. Breaking habits. What she'll do for work . . . if she *can* work. She can't sit around here all day. She'll go crazy."

"Well, she'll have ballet," I said. "That'll fill a lot of her time. Right?"

Mom took her hand off her eyes and stared at me like I had just suggested she take up unicorn training. "Abby. Blair's done with ballet."

Done? That was like saying the Earth was done spinning. Blair was made to dance.

Destiny, she'd said, placing her feet in her arch stretcher that looked like a torture device, not even wincing. *It's my destiny.*

"We'll figure it out. Don't you worry," said Mom. "We've got this. Hey. You okay?"

I stood up and yawned. "Tired."

"Go lie down until the pizza's here. This weather makes everyone sleepy."

The rain didn't let up. Every day there was more and more, leaving Dad running around patching leaks and Mom trying to find things for tourists to do inside, like the Moose Junction History Museum. *Woohoo*, come on in and see the largest musky ever caught in Fishtrap Lake! The gloves that *might* have belonged to the first settler who stumbled upon Musky River! Not exactly earth-shattering stuff, but Dad always said Mom could sell honey to bees. The only people who were happy were the fishermen, who insisted pike always bit more when it rained.

I went to the library most days, working my way through the fantasy series and gossiping with Harriet. I read and read and read; it was too cloudy to even use my telescope.

But I also kept scrolling through Sophie's and Lex's

Instagram feeds. I couldn't stop. *Scroll.* The two of them in rain jackets, standing in a puddle and laughing. *Scroll.* A bunch of girls from school, lying in sleeping bags and sticking their tongues out. *Scroll.* Sophie and Lex sharing a bucket of popcorn at the movie theater, where Jade said she'd seen them a few times. Those guys couldn't do anything without making sure everyone knew how much fun they were having. *Scroll.*

Later that week, I was helping Harriet put together a display for the library on books about space. As the eclipse got closer and closer, you could feel the energy in the air. The town was starting to get packed, even with the rain. A couple of national news stations had already arrived, ready to see the eclipse in all its glory. Harriet and I pulled books on everything from space fantasy to Carl Sagan to my very own Katherine Johnson. I put out *Goodnight Moon* and *Number the Stars* and the *Twilight* series, too.

I was standing back to admire our handiwork when I heard the door open behind me. I couldn't believe who I saw.

It was Dr. Leo Lacamoire himself, in a thick green raincoat with the hood up. It looked kind of ridiculous, to see such a stuffy guy in a raincoat with his hood pulled up, as if a hurricane was fast approaching and it was his job to report it.

"Hi there," said Harriet. "Can I help you find something today?"

Dr. Lacamoire stared at me as if he was sure he knew me from somewhere, but wasn't sure where.

"Hi, Dr. Lacamoire. It's me—Abby McCourt?" I reminded him. "I came over about the raccoon!"

He shook his head. "Yes! Yes. Of course. Hello."

We all stood there awkwardly. He glanced around, not moving.

"Um . . . sir? Can I help you find something?" Harriet repeated. "Something to cozy up with on this rainy day? Weatherman's finally predicting clear skies for tomorrow; thank goodness."

"No." He blinked. "Actually—what am I saying? Yes. I'm looking for archives of the local newspaper."

Harriet shook her head. "We don't have a newspaper in Moose Junction. Not much happens here. Waukegan County has a website, though, and they used to have a paper. *Waukegan Weekly*. All of the issues are archived online. I can give you the library's login if you'd like, and you can peruse on there."

"That would be lovely. Thank you." That accent

again, and words like *lovely*. He was about as out of place in Moose Junction as a vegetarian. I mean, no offense to plant eaters, but when you live in a town where people mainly come to kill things and eat them, you just sort of stick out. We consider jerky a food group.

"I'll get it for you," said Harriet, walking to her computer.

"Nice display," Dr. Lacamoire said, nodding toward the books. He picked up the one on Katherine Johnson and flipped through it.

"I did my oral report on her last year," I said. "She's kinda my hero."

He cracked a smile. "Really? Not Sally Ride? First woman in space, you know."

"Valentina Tereshkova was the first woman in space," I said, shaking my head. "Sally Ride was just American."

He laughed, in kind of a weird way—like a seal barking. "Well, you Americans usually claim everything you do as first, don't you?"

"*Besides*," I said. "Sally Ride couldn't have made it up there if Katherine Johnson hadn't done the math."

"But you want to sit behind a desk when you could be exploring the stars?" he asked, an eyebrow raised.

Sure. I was perfectly content behind a desk.

Most of the time.

"I can be up for adventure," I said. "But Katherine Johnson found the answers. She was like . . . a detective. She could find anything."

Dr. Lacamoire just looked at me, as if he were making some kind of decision in that very second. I just wasn't sure, standing there in the Moose Junction library, what exactly it was. I didn't know that Dr. Leo Lacamoire was looking for something, desperate to find it, on a quest of his very own—

No. I didn't know any of that, not then. All I knew was that this guy was quite possibly out of his mind.

"Anything," he repeated.

That *anything* said a million things.

"Well, I should—I should get going," I said, inching toward the door.

"See you later, Abby," said Harriet, handing Dr. Lacamoire an index card with a login code on it. "Stay dry."

I ducked out the door and ran home, both because Jade had stolen the only umbrella we had and because I had the creepy-crawly feeling that the mysterious astronomer was watching me go.

That night, as Dr. Leo Lacamoire sat on the computer

and pulled up archives, digging for a single photograph in a mountain of history, looking for things that were long ago lost, I helped Dad make dinner. I was just starting to set the table when the doorbell rang.

"Got it," yelled Mom, emerging from upstairs. "Man, that smells good, you two."

"Fried chicken is a gift from the Lord," said Dad, washing his hands. "We're unworthy." When Mom cooked, everything was perfectly measured: a teaspoon of this, half a cup of that. She wouldn't dare make dinner without a cookbook splayed open on the counter. Dad liked to crank up the Beatles and do dashes and sprinkles and handfuls; most of the time, we didn't even use recipes. Blair hated it. She'd ask him how much butter was in something and he'd say "a chunk."

Mom pulled open the door. Standing there, absolutely drenched, was Simone.

"Oh, gosh! Get in here, out of the rain," said Mom as Simone stepped in, shivering.

"Thank you. I'm sorry to intrude. Looks like you're about to eat," said Simone.

"Not a problem," Mom assured her. "Is there something I can help you with? Usually we ask guests to call the office if there's an issue. . . ." Mom had a cell phone that got office calls when nobody was manning the station.

"Yeah, I'm sorry. I would have. But I actually came to talk to your daughter," she said, nodding toward me. "Abby, right?"

Mom and Dad turned to me, surprised.

"My boss—Dr. Lacamoire? I know you've met, but not sure if you knew—he's pretty well known in his field. He's considered an expert in our solar system. He teaches at MIT."

MIT! The Massachusetts Institute of Technology was my dream of dreams. I couldn't imagine spending my entire day learning about the stars. It was pretty far away, but like I said earlier—the heart hopes. You can't stop it.

Whenever I felt a jolt of hope, though, I tried to stamp it back down. I'd seen what hope did to people. I'd seen Blair and the Joffrey collide. I'd seen beautiful things turn so ugly. *Hope* was Paris Forrester, a girl from elementary school who would smile sweetly so all the teachers liked her before making fun of them behind their backs. Hope looked like the hero of the story but it was usually the villain.

"Well, he'd heard that Abby had an interest in astronomy," said Simone. "Said he ran into you at the library?

He was wondering if she'd like to join us for dinner tomorrow night. Whole family is invited, of course. Not to brag, but I can cook a mean lasagna. Do you like Italian? We'd love to have you."

I remembered all those telescopes in his lookout.

"Yes!" I said instantly. "Can we?"

"That's very kind of Dr. Lacamoire," said Mom. "We would be honored."

"I also wanted to thank you for dealing with the raccoon issue so quickly. I know I came off a bit intense. Working for a scientist is something else," she said, shaking her head. "I didn't mean to make more work for you."

"No worries at all. Nobody wants an animal sneaking through their door at night. But dinner would be great," Dad said. "I actually have an interest in astronomy myself. Taught Abby everything she knows," he said, tugging on my ponytail.

"Great. Seven o'clock okay for you?" asked Simone. I nodded.

"I'll see you all tomorrow, then," she said. "I should get back."

As Simone ran out into the rain, Mom turned and stared at me. "Wow! That's pretty exciting, Abby. How generous of him."

I nodded again, and tried to calm the storm of thoughts running through my head. I tried to tie down that anticipation, that hope that was trying to fly like a bird. That wish for Dr. Leo Lacamoire and that lookout of telescopes to be my Summer Adventure, no matter how quirky he seemed. I didn't know when, and I didn't know how, but I wanted to be back in that lookout with those telescopes. *Goodbye, Katherine Johnson; hello, Sally Ride.* I wanted to observe the galaxy and see something beautiful—something other than pine trees and sisters who were sick.

But I clipped hope's wings. People say *hope* like it's a good thing, but they're kidding themselves. Hope is the monster that hides under your bed. It's the flame that burns down the house while you're sleeping.

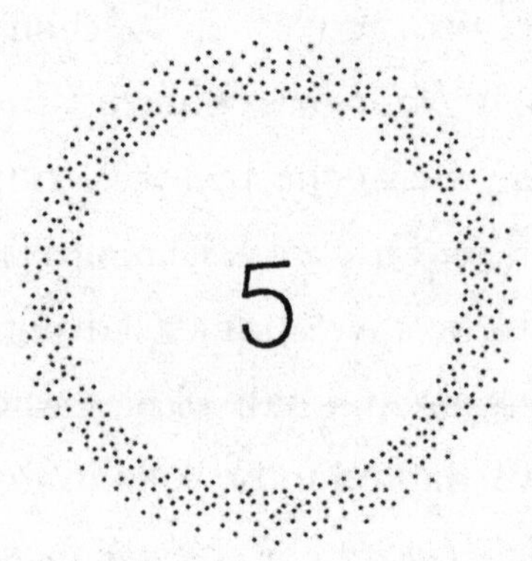

LAST APRIL

Twelve years old

Sixteen weeks before Simone showed up on our doorstep and invited me to dinner, Dr. Leo Lacamoire was in a deep hole. He was lying on his couch, unable to do anything worthwhile. He hadn't yet moved on to the *action* part of his plan; he was still in the *never-ending sorrow* part. He was eating a lot of fake orange snack foods—the foods of depression: Cheetos, Cheez-Its, cheddar-flavored potato chips. Foods you eat when you just don't care anymore.

It was the beginning of spring, and Waukegan County High was getting ready for senior prom. Blair was home-schooled and didn't do many of the typical high school things. Jade did enough for both of them. Blair was too busy for football games and homecoming parades and prom. She had a career she was preparing for. Her only friends were her dance mates, and she talked about them more like colleagues than soul sisters. They weren't exactly having sleepovers or doing BuzzFeed quizzes together. The only thing they probably shared was mutual judgment of each other for things like bending your knees during arabesques.

But Caleb Evers had asked her to the dance with a dozen red roses, and even my sister couldn't say no to that.

It was called *homeschooling*, but it wasn't like Mom sat Blair down and taught her precalculus or anything. Blair would just Skype with some woman named Sasha in Madison and go through tons of workbooks on her own. Mostly, she danced, even though after the Joffrey Incident, we weren't sure what her next steps were. She wouldn't be going to New York in the fall, like we'd all been planning. However, her coach, Aleksander, had enrolled her in a competition in July that could put her in front of some company eyes.

Mom hated Aleksander. I was surprised she didn't have a dartboard somewhere in the house with his picture pinned to it. She purposely wrote Blair's checks out to *Alexander* instead, her one small act of rebellion. I cheered silently every time she did it. I wasn't a fan of Aleksander, either; he was loud and kind of mean. He thought Blair didn't live up to her potential.

Things were bad. The Joffrey Incident had made them worse. We didn't know how bad, but if you stepped into our house, you could feel that everyone was tiptoeing around silently hoping everything would get better soon. Blair had started going to a small group for girls with "anxiety issues" on Tuesday nights. *You're too stressed*, I'd heard Mom say as they argued down in the kitchen one night. *It will help*. But I wasn't so sure it did. Blair hated it, coming home in a terrible mood and slamming her bedroom door so loud it made Obi jump. Every single mealtime was some kind of argument about ingredients and portion sizes and whether or not Mom had bought the low-calorie orange juice. One morning, Blair had woken up to find her scale gone, and she shrieked so loudly I thought the pine needles would fall from the trees. Mom and Dad hadn't fessed up to it, but I found it later that day, shoved at the bottom of the garbage can, broken into a million pieces. Every day was a new war.

On a Tuesday night when Blair was gone, the doorbell rang, and I was the only one home to answer it.

Standing there was Caleb Evers, who—look, I'll just say it. If you weren't a little bit in love with Caleb Evers, you were blind. He was tall and muscley, but not in a weird protein-shake way, with brown hair that flopped in his eyes a little bit, especially when he played drums. He probably helped little old ladies cross the street in his free time. Basically, he belonged in a movie. Definitely leading man material.

Caleb was in love with Blair, and that meant so much to me. Because it was getting harder and harder lately to see why Blair was so special. Memories of when she was my best friend were slipping away. The old, fearless Blair was being replaced with a crying, scared mess. Spending time with someone else who loved her reminded me. People who remembered that spark of life she brought into a room, and people who knew how kind and silly and adventurous she could be—those were the people I wanted her surrounded by. Not Aleksander and his critical glare, always measuring the arch of her feet and the height of her jump.

Blair let me hang out with her and Caleb, sometimes. One night, a month before prom, they'd taken me to a movie so we could visit Jade at work. She gave us huge buckets of popcorn for free, because even Jade loved

Caleb. Blair hadn't eaten a bite and reminded us that the movie theater shouldn't be allowed to call the butter flavoring *butter* because it's so fake. But Caleb and I had had competitions during the previews to see how many kernels in a row we could each catch in our mouths, while Blair narrated the entire thing in a sportscaster voice.

I wondered if he even remembered that.

"Hi!" I said, surprised. "Blair's not here."

He grinned. "Yeah, I know. I actually came to see you."

"*Me?*" I suddenly realized I hadn't washed my hair in three days, but whatever. It was fine. No big deal.

"Yeah, you. Or Jade or your parents. Are they here?"

I shook my head. "Mom's grocery shopping and Jade's with her friends. Dad's just in the office."

"That's okay. I can talk to you. Can I come in?"

I opened the door wider and Obi took that golden opportunity to dash outside, practically plowing Caleb over. He laughed. "Dumb dog. I *love* that dumb dog."

We went into the kitchen and sat down. I felt so grown up. Caleb was here to see *me*. But then I realized that he looked jumpy. He was glancing around a lot and playing with his hands. This wasn't some visit to ask what color Blair's prom dress was.

"What's going on?" I asked him.

Caleb leaned forward and stared at me, hard. Those eyes could burn a hole in you.

"Abby, I want to ask you a few questions, and I need you to tell the truth, okay? It's super important."

"Okay," I said nervously, like I was on one of those cop shows.

"Did you eat dinner with Blair last night?"

I thought of the night before. Dad made pasta; I remembered the spaghetti sauce on Obi's ear. Jade had argued with Mom about whether or not she could get her belly button pierced. I had extra meatballs.

"No," I said. "She said she was having dinner at your house." She had run out the door, talking on her phone, mouthing *Caleb's* to Mom.

Caleb pressed his hands on the table so hard his fingers turned white. "What about the night before? Monday? Think, Abby."

"I don't remember. . . ."

"It's really, really important. It was warm that day, remember?"

I did. Brats and hot dogs on the grill, dinner on the back porch. Blair going on a date with Caleb and borrowing Mom's earrings. She had a sweater on even though it was eighty degrees, a miracle for northern Wisconsin in April. She was so cold now, always shivering, putting more and more layers on, and draping a blanket over her shoulders the second she walked through the door.

"She said you and her were going to Fiorelli's. Date night, whatever."

Caleb stared at me, and I stared back, and there it was—the crashing realization that I had been lied to.

He put his head in his hands. I was worried he would start crying, but he just sat there for a minute.

"Crap, Abby," he said finally. "Crap."

When he finally looked back up, Caleb Evers looked sadder than I'd ever seen a person look.

"I have to talk to your mom, okay?" he said. "You tell her as soon as she gets home that she should call me. She has my phone number, I think. But I'll give it to you just in case." He grabbed my cell phone and typed it in. I stared at it when he was done. *Caleb Evers*, right there in my cell phone. God, Sophie and Lex would *lose* it.

I told Mom when she got back, and she went right into her room to call him. She stayed in there for a long time, even after she hung up. I knocked, but she told me she had a headache and needed to rest.

When Blair came home that night, I wondered if she could tell I had betrayed her. I tried to talk to her, but she was already getting ready for bed at eight o'clock.

"It's kind of early," I pointed out as she brushed her teeth. She shrugged. She was *always* tired, coming straight home from dance or therapy and curling up into bed. Instead of getting better at ballet, she seemed to be getting worse. I'd spied on her practicing pirouettes in her room, and she would lose her balance, frustrated, before just giving up.

"Did you get any further on *Planet Pirates*?" I asked. I was waiting for her next chapter. Princess Stardust was stuck on Mars. She was getting so cold waiting for Captain Moonbeard to save her that her skin was turning blue. Blair's drawings were getting sadder and sadder. She used to always be happy when she was drawing. It wasn't like ballet, where the pressure to be the best, get the leading role, and land a company job loomed over her like the Death Star. When she was drawing, she could be exactly who she was in the moment. It was the Blair I loved, not the one Anna Rexia had taken hostage.

"No, Abby. I don't have time," she snapped. "Between school and dance and that stupid shrink I can hardly breathe."

"Sorry," I said.

She sighed. "It's not your fault. *I'm* sorry. I just hate

these dumb sessions where they want you to talk about your feelings, blah blah blah." She waved her hand. "I need to be focused on this competition in July. It could be my last chance. Aleksander said someone from the Royal Ballet will be there. I have to be the best, you know?" She stared at herself in her bathroom mirror. "There's no room for error. I can't have another Joffrey meltdown."

I told on you to Caleb, I wanted to scream. I was pretty sure she'd have more therapy coming her way.

"Besides, prom is this weekend," said Blair. "Which means no weekend rehearsal time. Aleksander is so pissed . . . it's pretty stupid. Kind of a waste of time."

"It'll be so fun, though," I said excitedly. "Caleb in a tux, and you guys can slow dance. Maybe you'll be prom queen."

Blair barked out a laugh. I thought she was going to make fun of me, but instead she gave me a hug. I could feel her rib cage, like if I squeezed her too hard she'd shatter.

"I love you, Abs," she whispered into my ear. She sounded sad. But maybe a little hopeful, too.

That Saturday was the big day. Mom's college friend Amber came over to do Blair's hair. Originally, she wanted it down; she had it up so often for ballet that we all agreed she should try something new. But her hair was so thin. Amber ran a brush through it and a clump fell out. She glanced at Mom, then back at Blair.

"Sweetie, I love you, but your hair is brittle as candy," she said. "It has to go up."

Amber was a miracle worker, maneuvering Blair's hair up in a French twist. Her dress was pink—not Barbie doll pink, but a soft pink—long and flowing with a few sparkles down the skirt. She looked like a princess. She looked like a princess *all* the time, at a bajillion dance recitals, but this was different. She actually looked *happy*, not anxious. Like she wasn't worrying about pointing her toes. Instead of being caked in stage makeup, she just wore a little mascara and lip gloss. We locked Obi in the basement so he wouldn't jump on her. When Caleb came to pick her up, Mom took so many pictures her phone ran out of memory. Even Jade stuck around for a bit before going to meet up with her friends.

"You be careful, okay?" Mom said nervously, gripping Blair as if she were sending her off to war.

"I will, Mom. I promise," she said.

We all felt it, watching Blair and Caleb drive off. Hope. The feeling that maybe things were on the upswing.

Maybe Blair was getting better. Maybe she could be a normal girl tonight, a fairy princess at the prom, and then she'd dance beautifully at the competition this summer and get offered a spot in the Royal Ballet. Maybe we could all go to London to see her and try to spot Will and Kate.

That *hope*: it can wrap you up so tightly. You think it's giving you a hug when really it's strangling you.

Mom and Dad and I watched an old black-and-white movie on TV and went to bed. I hated trying to sleep when Jade wasn't there, but she had just gotten her job at the movie theater and had to work more weekends than not.

I must have drifted off eventually, though, because the next thing I knew, Mom was shaking me.

"Abigail. Abigail! Wake up!"

"Geez, what?" I rubbed my eyes and glanced at my phone. It was 12:34. I still remember that.

"Blair's been in an accident," she said. I sat up quickly. I realized Mom had been crying. I'd never seen my mom cry in my entire life, not even at my grandma's funeral in second grade. Mom didn't cry. She was our moon, tugging us all into orbit when we spun out of control.

"What? What happened? Is she okay?"

"They think so. The doctor's checking for a concussion. She's at Memorial Hospital all the way in Cedar Valley. There was a car accident. Daddy and I are going and Jade slept over at Cassidee's, so you're by yourself, okay?"

"By myself?" I asked meekly. Sure, Mom and Dad let me stay home alone. I was twelve. But not in the middle of the night.

"Obi's downstairs and wide awake. We'll lock all the doors and be home in the morning. You'll be fine. Okay? We need to go. *Now*."

As if Obi was a guard dog. If a robber showed up, Obi would probably lick his feet and turn over for a belly rub. But I just nodded. Mom ran down the stairs and I heard the truck start up and take off.

Somehow, I managed to fall asleep, even though I was picturing Blair lying mangled in a hospital bed. A few hours later, I woke up to Jade coming in, shutting the door hard behind her. The sun was up.

"Hey. Mom just called. They're on the way home."

I sat up again, rubbing sleep out of my eyes. "What *happened*?"

Tough Jade, Can't-Hurt-Me Jade, Don't-Mess-With-Me Jade looked tiny. She sat on my bed and pulled her knees up to her chest. "Caleb was at the hospital, too. He got in a fight with Blair after a party or something, Mom said. Blair wanted to drive home to calm down. Caleb's car is totally ruined . . . they hit a tree? Or a log? I don't even know."

"Was she drinking?" I mean, please. They teach you not to do that in kindergarten now.

"No. I think it was dark and she probably hadn't eaten anything in four days and was an idiot and blacked out," said Jade.

"God, Jade! Why do you have to be so *mean*? She's in the *hospital*."

"Why do you have to be so *stupid*? You're twelve years old. Wake up," snapped Jade.

I hated her then. I hated her with everything in me. I didn't even know it was possible to feel that kind of hate.

"She's trying," I said angrily.

"Wow, yeah, she's really *trying*. Caleb told Mom everything. About how Blair's been lying about dinner. About how he found those stupid lunches Mom has been packing her to take to dance all stuffed in her closet! She's throwing her entire life away and you're like, *la-di-dah, Blair's perfect, whatever, everything's fine*. She could have killed somebody in that car. Someone could be dead. *She* could be dead!"

"Go away," I spat out.

"Grow up," she snapped back.

I jumped off my bed and left our room, slamming the door behind me.

Blair, my hero Blair, the Princess Stardust of my real life. Blair who could dance on her toes and perform in front of hundreds of people. Blair, who crumpled up bad guys and stomped them under her feet. That was what I had *thought*, our whole lives. Had Blair changed, or was this—this liar, this sneaky person, this sick girl—who she'd been all along? Maybe I had never known her at all.

Do you want to know the worst thing in the entire world? When you've hoped that hope, let it fly, but then watch it get shot to the ground. When it's ashes at your feet. When Anna Rexia does fouettés and piqué turns on those ashes, laughing as she spins at how you could have ever been so stupid as to think things were better than they truly were.

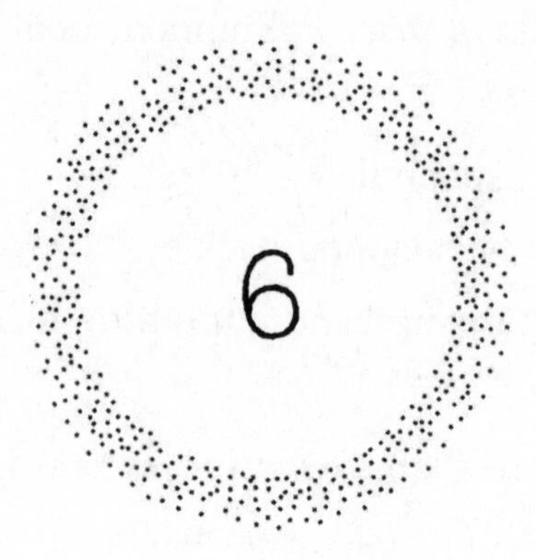

AUGUST, PRESENT DAY

Twelve years old

I was up all night googling Dr. Leo Lacamoire.

Or should I say: Dr. Leo Lacamoire, PhD, professor of astronomy and astrophysics, graduate of Oxford University, special interest in detecting and characterizing extrasolar planets, world-renowned expert on gamma-ray bursts. Visitor to the White House on three separate occasions, featured expert on the National Geographic channel, History Channel, and Weather Channel. Guest star on some comedy show about nerdy geniuses. Had his own Netflix special. Author of countless studies and three books, including *ExtraPlanets: Looking for Life*

Beyond Our Solar System, which was dedicated to his editor, Joanna Creech.

Dr. Leo Lacamoire had given a TED Talk on finding new planets. I watched it four times. He strode across the stage in dress pants and a white shirt, waving his arms around but talking very intensely.

"The key to finding new planets isn't finding the planet itself. It's finding things *affected* by that planet. Planets can't act in isolation. Astronomers will notice gravitational pulls, changes in light color, or a shadow dimming the light of a nearby star. Planets are not solitary beings; they affect the world around them in—pardon my pun—astronomical ways." The audience chuckled. Then he gripped the podium and leaned in, which I could already notice was his trademark *serious-business* move.

"When we're looking for a new planet, we don't look for a new planet. We look for the things around it changing. We look for its effect on the world. It's only a matter of time before a planet makes itself known."

I wanted nothing more right then than to look through my telescope, but it was still insanely cloudy. I shut my laptop and pulled my notebook out from under my bed, feeling my hand brush against a library book I thought

I'd lost and a few more of Abby's Life Artifacts. What's beneath someone's bed can sometimes tell you a lot about them. Blair had piles of old pointe shoes she couldn't make herself throw away. Jade had dirty clothes she was too lazy to bring to the laundry room. This notebook was where I usually wrote *Planet Pirates* drafts before adding the final version to our actual project. Sometimes I had nightmares of dying in some catastrophe and someone finding the crappy stories I'd written in it. *Ha! She thought she had such talent*, they would chuckle at my funeral. *She should have stuck to stargazing.*

I curled up in bed with my notebook, but I couldn't even write. I needed Blair's drawings first. That was how we did it. I felt sad for Princess Stardust, lonely and stuck. I wanted her to hurry up and be saved.

Jade burst into the room, smelling like popcorn. She saw what I was holding.

"I thought you two were done with your stories," she said, peering over my shoulder.

I closed it. "Just looking."

She rolled her eyes. "You're going to be carrying that thing around when you go to college. When the Sugar Plum Fairy's on Broadway or whatever."

My face got hot and I shoved the notebook back under

the bed. "Jealous. You still draw stick figures."

"Right. Like I don't have better things to do than draw stupid aliens. I have a job. And friends. Unlike you."

"They're not stupid!"

She reached over and turned the light off. "Stop living in la-la land and go to sleep."

As we walked to Eagle's Nest the next evening to have dinner with Dr. Leo Lacamoire, all I could think about was that TED Talk. To spend your day finding new planets sounded like the coolest thing ever. He had to be here for the eclipse.

I lifted my hand to knock on the door, but it swung open. Standing there was Simone, in jeans and a black T-shirt.

"Saw you coming," she said cheerfully, kicking the door the rest of the way open. She had an oven mitt on. "I hope you're hungry."

"We certainly are," Mom assured her.

"Shoes off?" asked Dad as we stepped in.

"That would be great. He's kind of a neat freak," she whispered. We kicked off our shoes and walked farther into the foyer, where we heard the music. More classical. Those rising and falling violins made you feel like you were at the ballet. Blair would never eat lasagna. Pasta plus cheese plus buttery bread equals Blair's Worst Nightmare.

As if she could read my mind, Simone asked where my sister was. Mom, Dad, and I looked at each other, kind of surprised. Had news about Blair really made it to them already?

"The blonde? She's your sister, right?" asked Simone, confused.

"Oh. *Jade.* Yes. She actually had to work," Mom said. "At the movie theater in town?"

"That's too bad. The movie theater, huh? I worked at one of those in high school. Always came home smelling like popcorn," she said, leading us into the dining room.

"Abigail McCourt!" a voice crowed. It was Dr. Leo Lacamoire, descending the staircase two steps at a time and lowering the volume on the speakers with his phone. "There she is. Astronomer, seventh grader, avid library aficionado."

"Eighth grader in the fall," I said.

He waved a hand, as if such a detail couldn't matter less to him. "Yes, yes. Welcome. What can Simone get you all to drink? Water, soda, iced tea? Wine for those of us old enough to partake? I wasn't sure what you liked. . . ."

Simone opened the fridge to every kind of juice and soda imaginable. Bottles of Coke and orange juice and lemonade and Mountain Dew all clinked together in the door.

"Water's actually fine for me," I said.

"Sparkling? Berry flavored?" The doctor bounced on his toes. Where had he gotten all this stuff? You definitely couldn't buy berry-flavored water at Coontail's.

"Um . . . tap?"

"You're freaking them out," hissed Simone, grabbing a cup from the cupboard and filling it at the sink. "Relax."

Mom and Dad glanced at each other, and I could read their minds: *What in the world?*

"Yes! Everything is grand," Dr. Lacamoire assured me, pouring two glasses of dark red wine and handing them to my parents. "Simone has whipped up a feast fit for kings."

Dr. Lacamoire took my dad and me upstairs to check out his telescopes while Simone finished getting dinner ready and chatted with my mom. He had five of them, all on tripods, pointed outside at different angles.

"Whoa," I breathed, running my hand over the largest one. "This is a Tyler-Weimer. They're like, eight bajillion dollars."

"Abigail," Dad hissed.

Dr. Lacamoire smirked. "Not quite eight bajillion. But close."

"Wow," Dad said, admiring his setup. "This is amazing."

"You're all set for the eclipse, huh?" I asked him. "Did you get your glasses already? I've had mine for weeks."

He snorted and pulled out what looked like binoculars. "These are sunoculars. Specifically designed for eclipse viewing. They're what I always use."

"You've seen a total eclipse before?" I asked, my jaw dropping. "That's, like, a once-in-a-lifetime thing!"

"Nonsense. They happen once every two years or so. I usually just need to travel. I've observed total eclipses in Bangladesh, Auckland, and Tokyo—but never here in the U.S."

"Careful with those," Dad warned me as Dr. Lacamoire handed over the sunoculars.

I turned them over in my hand. "These are *sweet.*"

"And *expensive,*" he said, plucking them back out from my hands. Then he looked nervous. "But—if you'd like to see them— I'm sorry, I shouldn't have—"

"Dinner!" hollered Simone.

Dr. Lacamoire looked thankful for our interruption.

"Come then, Abigail, Gary. Dinner is served. After, when it's darker, you can look through the Tyler-Weimer if you'd like."

"That would be amazing. And it's Abby," I told him. "Just Abby."

The thing about lasagna is that you always eat more than you mean to. Pasta in general, really. You can't just eat a normal-person amount; you have to eat, like, three helpings. I wished I had leggings on.

"Ugh," Simone groaned, clearing the table. "Carb overload."

"It was delicious, though," Mom said.

"There's ice cream, too, but I can't eat another bite," said Simone. "Anyone need some sugar?"

"I'm stuffed," I admitted. "I don't think I could fit it in."

"Coffee?" she asked my parents.

"I think I'm okay," said Mom, and Dad nodded in agreement.

"Abby? No, what am I saying. You're twelve."

"My best friend Sophie drinks coffee," I said. "But it's mainly flavored creamer." My best friend. Ha. She was about as much my best friend as the bus driver was now.

"Well then," said Dr. Lacamoire, "let's make ourselves

more comfortable, shall we?" The guy was being *weird.* He was jittery, asking us questions with wide eyes and then interrupting with new ones halfway through. He wanted to know when my parents moved here, when they opened up the resort, when the library was built . . . it was like his mind was constantly sparking off in new directions. He was never fully paying attention to what anyone was saying. And he'd barely touched his food, but the rest of us had eaten enough to make up for it.

We went into the living room. My parents and I sat on the leather couch, which my mom had spent months picking out from Crafting the Woods, and Dr. Lacamoire delicately slid into the armchair. Dad kept glancing around, and I could tell it made him feel weird to be in one of his own cabins as a guest instead of there to fix a toilet.

The office cell phone suddenly rang.

"Sorry," Mom sighed, pulling it out. "We're completely booked this month, so things have been a little crazy. I should take this."

She stepped back toward the kitchen, murmuring into the phone, while Dad and Simone chatted about the best places to grab breakfast in town. Dr. Lacamoire and I sat there awkwardly.

"I've been trying to get that fireplace going," he said, nodding to it, "but I can't find the switch. I wouldn't think we'd even need a fireplace in August, but goodness, that nighttime air can bite through the windows."

"The switch?"

"To turn it on. Do you know where it is? It's one of your houses, after all."

"Um . . ." Making stupid people not feel stupid was one of my specialties. Trevor King had been my lab partner last year, and let's just say he wasn't the reason we got an A-. "There is no switch, sir. Although it'd be great if there were. You have to take wood from out back and set it on fire."

"Oh my goodness, really? I assumed all fireplaces were electric now. This is a quaint little town, isn't it?"

I smiled. "Sure is. Do you want me to show you how to get one started? I'm a pro."

"No, no. Unnecessary. But, er, now that you mention it . . ." He glanced at Simone and my dad, who was showing her a photo of a restaurant on his phone. "There's something you *can* help me with."

Mom suddenly burst back into the room, looking frazzled. "I'm incredibly sorry, but we're going to need to cut the evening a bit short. Gary, that was J.J. The guests in

Robin's Egg apparently decided to go on a little joyride without a boating license. And with beer. And no concept of how to follow buoys to avoid rocks on the lake."

Dad groaned. "This is why next summer, we're not accepting any bachelor parties."

"We need to handle this. One of us should go help J.J. haul the boat out, and one of us needs to drive the boys back to the cabin."

"Thank you so much for having us," Dad said. "Sorry about this."

"But I didn't get to look in the Tyler-Weimer!" I burst out. I couldn't leave without looking through the telescope, and a few stars were finally starting to peek out.

"Another night," Mom promised me.

"But . . ." Dr. Lacamoire glanced at Simone, a look on his face. Worry? Fear?

"If you all don't mind, I'd be happy to walk Abby back if she wants to stick around and take a look through the scope," said Simone.

Mom and Dad looked at each other.

"I'd hate for her to be a bother," said Dad.

"Um, I'm right here," I said.

"Not a bother at all!" Dr. Lacamoire assured them.

"Ten minutes," said Mom, pointing at me. "Then get

out of their hair. Text me when you're home. And Obi needs to go out."

"Ten minutes," I repeated back.

"Whoa."

It was like when you didn't realize how dirty and sunscreen-smeared your sunglasses were until you wiped them off. I'd never seen the stars so clearly, sprinkled across the sky as if by design.

"Can you spot Aquila? Seems appropriate, given the name of our cabin," said Dr. Lacamoire. "*Eagle.* Start with—"

"Altair," I said, fixing the telescope on one of the brightest stars in the sky.

"Wow," said Simone, organizing some papers on the desk. "You really do know your stars."

"My dad takes me out stargazing a lot," I said. "He would love this."

"You'll have to bring him back a different night. He's more than welcome," said Dr. Lacamoire. He leaned forward, his eyes affixed out the window. But once again, he wasn't looking at the stars. He was looking back across the lake.

"Thanks for showing this to me," I said.

"You know what I love about the stars, Abigail?" said Dr. Lacamoire.

"Abby."

He continued. "They're a sort of map. They let you know where you are in the world. There are constellations we can see here that they can't see in Antarctica right now, or in Ethiopia. And if you go on a sailing trip across the ocean, the stars can guide you the entire way."

"It's pretty amazing," I agreed.

We stood in silence, me looking through the telescope and him gazing out the window, until Simone spoke up.

"For cripes' sake, Leo, get on with it," she said, rolling her eyes. "I got her here. I made her *dinner*. I'm not doing this part for you."

"What?" I asked, confused.

Simone pointed at him. "We could have stayed in Cambridge. Had a nice, relaxing summer. Done some press for the eclipse, worked on your book. But no. You had a *quest*. I told you, she's the best person to help with it."

"She's a child," snapped Dr. Lacamoire.

"Uh, she's right here," I said.

And then, Dr. Leo Lacamoire did his signature thing. He leaned forward, ever so slightly, staring out the window as if he were looking for one of his new planets. The key to a new galaxy, out there spinning among the stars.

"Abigail," he said slowly, "I'm on a quest. And you may be the only one who can help me."

"*Me?*" I asked, surprised. Because as much as I'd felt like Dr. Leo Lacamoire was *my* summer adventure, that this MIT professor and brilliant astronomer was going to unlock some kind of new world right here in Moose Junction, it's not like I thought it would actually happen. I thought summer would come and go, the tourists breezing in and out with their sunscreen and fishing licenses, the eclipse blazing across the sky and a million eyes glancing up. And then Dr. Leo Lacamoire would be gone, back out east where he came from to find new planets out there in the sky. And I would stay here, in a dot, in northern Wisconsin. Friendless. Sisterless. Like something drifting around in space.

A word like *quest* sounded a lot like *destiny*. And that was a word I wanted nothing to do with.

"The library," he said, turning to look at me. "Moose Junction Library. You go there a lot. Nearly every day. You're friends with the librarian."

"Well, yeah. There's not a lot to do here when it rains."

"No! It's more than that. You love that place. I can tell." He tapped his forehead. "I'm a professor. I notice things that other people miss. The library is special to you. You know it very, very well."

That was true. The library—to me, it meant peace. *Escape*, a one-way ticket out of the world's smallest town. I could read words from people who understood loneliness and heartbreak, those big feelings that were so hard to put into words. I didn't have a Big Summer Adventure, but I could make one of my own on those beanbag chairs. It was my favorite building in the entire world.

I nodded.

"This sounds ludicrous." He shook his head. "But listen to me. Twenty years ago, something was buried in front of the library. It was a Moose Junction time capsule, to be rediscovered in one hundred years."

A *time capsule.*

I raised an eyebrow. "Really?"

"Yes. All kinds of things were buried in it. Baseball cards, pressed flowers . . ." He waved a hand in the air, as if to say *nonsense.* "But also! A telescope."

I froze.

"Why would someone put a telescope in a time

capsule?" I asked. What good was a machine meant for looking at the sky buried underground?

"Not just any telescope. A Star-Gazer Twelve."

A Star-Gazer Twelve wasn't a telescope. It was a magic wand. It made stars and planets feel as if they were inches away. I'd never seen one in my life, except at the planetarium in Chicago during our fifth-grade field trip there. I hadn't even looked through it; it was just part of some demonstration. Trevor King had been making fart noises every time the astronomer bent over to look through it.

I must have made a face, because he smiled proudly.

"Aha! Yes, I knew you were the girl for the job," Dr. Lacamoire said, beaming. "I told you, Simone, didn't I? I told you! The girl is smart! She knows her telescopes! She knows the importance of seeing what is out there in the world and *understanding* it!"

"I believe *I* told *you*," said Simone flatly.

I shook my head. "I'm sorry, I don't . . . I don't understand."

Dr. Leo Lacamoire crossed his arms, cool as a cucumber. All his plans were falling into place. His research was finally paying off.

"We're going to find where that time capsule is buried.

We're going to dig it up. And we're going to restore that Star-Gazer Twelve to its rightful owner."

"Who?" I asked.

"Me."

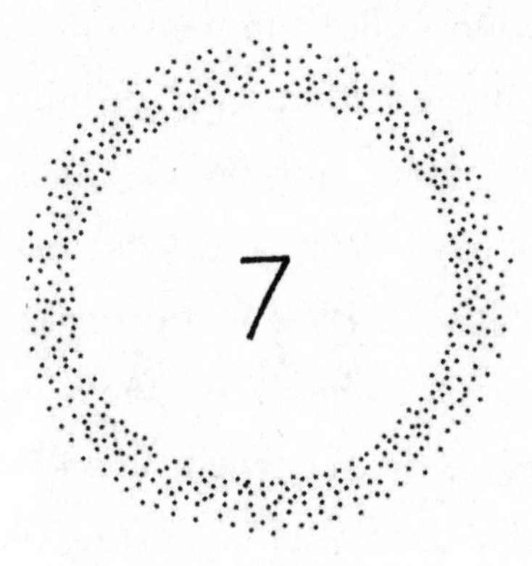

LAST JANUARY

Twelve years old

Almost seven months before Dr. Leo Lacamoire reeled me in with garlic bread and invited me to join his quest, before he nearly shed a tear over the disappearance of his beloved Star-Gazer Twelve and hatched a plot that would return it to its rightful owner, Blair had the biggest audition of her life.

The Joffrey Ballet School Trainee Program was a four-year apprenticeship meant to take devoted ballerinas and turn them into superstars. After the program, they'd be whisked away to Paris or Moscow or Los Angeles and dance with the most elite companies in the world. They would stretch higher, bend further, and point longer. They would be molded into professionals, after dancing for eight hours a day for four long years in New York City.

The Joffrey was all Blair had ever wanted since she was a little kid. For as long as I could remember, Blair had been dancing, first at Sweet Toes Ballet School in downtown Cedar Valley before getting plucked out and put on a real company team in Milwaukee. Aleksander planted the Joffrey seed and steadily watered it, letting it grow and grow like a weed that took over her whole brain. She'd get wide-eyed, talking about it and pulling up photos of the Joffrey dancers. All of them so tall, elegant, strong.

Thin.

Our family was always so excited about When Blair's in New York. We'd all go to the Macy's Thanksgiving Day Parade. We'd see the Rockefeller Tree lighting. It seemed so *sure*, as if we had looked into a crystal ball and sealed the future ages ago. But that feeling was getting further and further way. The Joffrey was becoming less a plan and more of a desperate hope we were all clinging to. Like if only Blair could get into Joffrey and go to New York, all her issues would magically disappear.

She couldn't be in such a competitive program if she was sick, so obviously, she would get better. This wasn't just another recital or competition. This was her dream. *This is everything I've worked for*, Blair would say, staring in the mirror.

The audition tour was making a pit stop in Chicago, and Aleksander had secured Blair a spot. She would be taking a class from a Joffrey instructor while another one took notes on everything from the size of her head to the point of her toes. Blair couldn't just be great, she had to be *the best*; spots were limited and she needed to land a scholarship, too. I helped her count fouettés at night in her room—forty-seven, forty-eight, forty-nine—until she collapsed on her bed in a pile of exhaustion.

In the fall, Blair was in her company's production of *Giselle*, playing Myrtha, queen of the ghostly spirits. She'd been so disappointed that she hadn't gotten the role of Giselle, but Myrtha was still known as one of the hardest parts to dance in all of classical ballet. Her performance was supposed to be stunning and spooky. Instead, it seemed like she couldn't stretch as high or keep her legs as straight as she used to. She even tripped out of her final arabesque, and she sobbed about it on the car ride home.

You were amazing, Mom had promised her, and she was. But nobody said that she stole the show.

After her Myrtha performance, Blair became even more obsessed with getting into the Joffrey. Everything seemed to hang on this one audition, this one moment. It was the reason for her extra rehearsal time in Milwaukee, the reason for her new leotards, and the reason she had to wake up at 5:00 a.m. every morning to do stretches. It was her Get Out of Jail Free Card, too. Blair didn't have to help in the office *because she had to practice*. Blair was allowed to snap at Mom and Dad because *she was stressed about her audition*. She didn't have to do homework because *she needed to focus on Chicago*. If I so much as rolled my eyes at Mom, I was sent to my room, but Blair could stomp around like the entire world was against her and we were all just supposed to nod sympathetically. Even I was starting to get annoyed.

Blair had begun therapy soon after landing her Myrtha role because talking to someone "would help with her stress," Mom had told Jade and me, but I knew it was really because Blair was disappearing inch by inch. Every time I hugged her, there was less to put my arms around. Weeks before the Joffrey audition, however, she stopped going. Apparently she *didn't have time when she needed to be perfecting her grand jeté.* She wasn't even answering phone calls from Caleb.

The night before we left for Chicago, Dad and I watched some baseball movie on Netflix.

"Hey, Dad?" I asked as some actor stepped up to bat.

"Yeah?"

"Do you think Blair's okay?" I don't know why I brought it up just then. Maybe it was that hope, taunting me. Maybe it was the possibility that things really *could* be okay.

He didn't move an inch or look away from the TV, but I know he heard me.

"Dad."

"Why do you ask, Abs?"

"She's just . . . she's sad, Dad. She's sad all the time."

He sighed, pausing the movie. "Blair is one of the strongest people I know, even if she's not behaving that way right now. But I think things are on the up and up. I do. Everything will be okay once she gets into the Joffrey."

Look, I wanted to scream. *Look at Blair. Look in her eyes. Nobody is looking.* The spotlight on her was blinding. She was a whirl of tutus and toe shoes, disappearing into the wind.

"It's my job to worry about your sister. It's your job to be a kid. Okay? We've got this." He reached over and patted my knee. "She will be just fine."

Just fine, like a Band-Aid over the blisters on Blair's feet. *Just fine.* But not fine. Not fine at all.

"You guys still doing your comic thing?" Dad asked. "She always loves that."

"Yeah," I said. "We are. Sometimes."

"Good." He flipped the TV back on, exhaling. "If we keep going like we believe things will work out, then they will, I think."

We watched the fake team lose and the fake coach learn some fake life lesson, neither of us thinking about baseball anymore. We were Blair's corps de ballet, dancing behind her in unison.

Our whole family rode down to Chicago the next day in my dad's truck. It was supposed to be a family vacation—*whoop-de-do*—the farthest place we'd gone in ages. But we weren't exactly feeling the Happy Family vibes. For weeks leading up to the trip, every night at dinner Blair would get all testy with Mom about whether or not she bought the low-fat yogurt, and why her chicken had to be cut into a million pieces, and *my stomach hurts, you're so mean, leave me alone, I'm not a kid*. Lately, everything with Blair and food had been an argument. It was like when Jade and I babysat Meggie Saunders across the lake, begging her to eat dinner and promising a later bedtime in exchange for some vegetables. Mom had to police Blair, giving her the third degree: *Did you even take a bite? What did you have for lunch? What about protein?* Jade rolled her eyes so much they were practically stuck that way. We were all getting frustrated with her. Open mouth, insert food, swallow. Blair got straight As. She knew how to eat. This shouldn't be that hard.

On the way to Illinois, Blair sat with her headphones in while I wrote for *Planet Pirates* and Jade texted some guy with a nose ring. Our entire family was nervous, full of audition anxiety, even though Blair would be the one dancing. It's like we all sensed something bad was going to happen. It felt kind of like we were marching toward our doom, like Harry going to see Voldemort when he knew He Who Must Not Be Named was just going to kill him. We were going to stay in a hotel, though, which we almost never got to do, and Mom said she would go swimming with me since Blair had to go to bed early, so I tried to keep a positive attitude. I imagined Blair in New York, riding the subway in her leg warmers like a scene in her favorite ballet movie. My optimism lifted weights, getting ready for battle. It was the underdog in that car.

After we arrived at the hotel and checked in, we ordered room service. Mom told Blair she needed to eat to keep her strength up for the audition in the morning, but they got in a big fight. Mom had asked Blair to finish her turkey burger and Blair had burst into tears. My fearless sister, the Performer, the Tough One, the Athlete. Queen of double-dog dares and *oh yes I can*. Crying over a chunk of *meat*.

To get us out of the drama, Dad took Jade and me swimming instead. I thought Jade would sit on her phone the whole time, but she actually went down the water slide with me, both of us racing to see who could go faster. We floated on our backs and she told me about Nose Ring Dude, who she didn't really like but just needed for a date to the Valentine's Day dance. I didn't say much, because it felt like a spell I could break. Jade talking to me, besides calling me a nerd or telling me I needed a life? It gave that optimism of mine another jolt, kicking his treadmill up a few notches.

The next morning, we walked Blair to her tryout. Chicago in late January is not a great place to be. The snow is all dirty and brown, with everyone's Christmas trees already dragged off by garbage trucks, and the cold is there to stay. There were soggy ice patches on every sidewalk, and Blair, as she had reminded us a thousand times, *couldn't fall and break an ankle before the biggest audition of her life.*

When we got to the theater, we were informed by a guy in all black checking people in that we weren't allowed to watch Blair try out. It was as if we were dropping her off at CIA headquarters for an interrogation. We waved goodbye, but she didn't wave back; she just disappeared in her leotard and pink tights, clutching her pointe shoes. Dad went to the hotel bar to watch some basketball game. I wanted to go to the planetarium or the Museum of Science and Industry, but Mom and Jade wanted to go shopping, so that's what we did.

We were arguing over a scarf when Mom got the call.

"It's so sparkly," said Jade. "It's not you at all."

"It could be me," I insisted. "I could be sparkly!"

"Gold sequins? Are you a Barbie doll? I thought you were some science genius. Look, this one has stars on it, at least."

"That is pretty cool. . . ."

Mom's phone went off, quacking like a duck, which made us crack up. Jade was always changing Mom's ringtone when she wasn't looking. She was still funny Jade, silly Jade, make-everyone-laugh Jade when she wanted to be. Mom laughed, too, until she saw it was Blair.

"Hello? Blair? Are you done already?" She glanced back at her phone, and I knew what she was thinking—we weren't supposed to be picking her up for another hour and a half.

"Blair." Serious voice. "I can't understand you, sweetie. Slow down. Take a breath."

Jade kept babbling about some feather earrings. But I was watching my mom's face. It crumpled.

"Oh, sweetie. Oh, my girl. Okay. You know what? It's okay. We'll be there in five minutes. Sit tight." She threw her phone back in her purse. "Girls, come on. We need to pick up your sister."

"Already?" asked Jade. "I thought we were gonna get lunch."

"Jade. *God.* Something's wrong, obviously," I said.

She rolled her eyes, slamming the feather earrings back on the counter. "Oh, sorry, I didn't get the memo that the world was revolving around Sugar Plum Fairy again."

"Girls, I cannot handle a fight right now," snapped

Mom. "I just can't. So shut it and follow me."

Back at the theater, we found Blair shaking and crying, as she told my mom in whispers what had happened. One of the women with Joffrey was there with her. She had white skin, blue hair, and sad eyes, looking at my sister, who was unraveling like an old sweater.

Sorry, she told my mom. They can't allow redos. Maybe next year. Maybe with a little more training.

Blair was like a car without enough gas. She couldn't point her toes, she couldn't leap in the air, she couldn't move like a flower petal. She was tired and gray, like the snow on the ground. She had fainted halfway through the class. The Joffrey people had almost called an ambulance.

The whole car ride back to Moose Junction, my dad listened to the basketball game on the radio and Blair leaned against the window and pulled her sweatshirt hood over her face. Her shoulders shook, and when we stopped for lunch, she didn't get anything and Mom didn't push her.

All the maybe-just-maybe excitement was gone. Our fears had been confirmed. It had been complete and utter defeat. There would be no Joffrey Trainee Program for Blair. She wouldn't be dancing with a professional company. She wouldn't be living in New York City. She wouldn't be doing anything at all.

Anna Rexia was rubbing Blair's back and singing to her while the rest of us plugged our ears and closed our eyes.

In the weeks after her failed audition, Mom and Dad tried hard to get Blair to think about next year.

"Sweetie, you can major in dance almost anywhere these days," Mom reminded her as they sat in the living room, surrounded by college brochures. Mom had put out a bowl of chips but Blair hadn't touched a single one "Even UW has a dance major."

"Great," she groaned. "I can major in dance at a Big Ten school while the kids at Joffrey and Julliard have actual careers. I can shake my butt at basketball games and minor in business and wind up selling insurance. Wow, what a life. How lucky am *I*."

"Chicago, then. Columbia College has a ballet program. . . ."

"Yeah, for losers who can't get in anywhere real!" She started tearing up. Blair was constantly crying these days, like the leaky faucet in Spruce, our oldest cabin. The house being five degrees colder than usual or Obi getting hair on her bed could set her off. We tiptoed around her like we were ballerinas ourselves.

"Maybe it's for the best, Blair," Mom said. "Maybe ballet—"

"You hate ballet, Mom," she snapped. "I got the memo."

"I don't hate ballet!"

"You do! You've always hated it! You want me to fail. You want me to spend the rest of my life renting out cabins to doctors from Iowa. Well, guess what? I have a dream. I have a *passion*. I'm not just *quitting ballet*!"

Mom slammed her hands on the table, pushed her chair out, and went upstairs. Dad followed behind. He squeezed Blair's shoulder as he walked around her. I went over to my big sister and looked at the shiny brochures.

"Maybe you should do art," I suggested. "You're good at drawing."

Blair sighed and yanked on my ponytail, wiping her eyes. "Oh, Abby. You don't *get* these things. You're just a kid."

This was something that eternally bugged me. *Just a kid.* Like kids were stupid. Like we couldn't *know* things. I knew plenty of things. I knew that Minnesota called itself the Land of 10,000 Lakes even though Wisconsin had more. I knew that the sun was actually a star and 400 times larger than the moon. I knew that Saturn would float if you put it in water. I knew that the Stormtrooper hitting his head in *Star Wars: A New Hope* was actually an accident but they left it in.

And I knew my mom really *did* hate ballet. She hated it when she wrote the huge checks for new tutus, she hated Aleksander and how snobby he was, and she hated how often we had to go to Milwaukee. But mostly she hated what it did to Blair. How my sister would make a mistake in rehearsal and cry for hours. How when she didn't get the lead in *Giselle* last year she hadn't come out of her room for two days. How she stretched so far it seemed as if she would break. How she was forgetting how to eat—first a little here and there, now entire meals, soon entire days. How she would walk by mirrors and suck in her cheeks. The way she would grab handfuls of side fat that weren't there. How she was disappearing into thin air.

"Here," I said, handing her our *Planet Pirates* book. "Your turn."

"Thanks, Abby," she said. "I need a little fantasy in my life right about now." She smiled, and I exhaled as if

I'd been holding my breath all day. That one small smile felt so important to me. Life wasn't over, even though there would be no Joffrey. We'd still have our comic, as small as it could seem.

"Are you dorks having a lovefest?" Jade bounded into the kitchen, opening the fridge, headphones in. "It's like the Hallmark Channel in here."

"Aww, feel left out?" said Blair. "Come be our bestest friend, Jadey-Pants." She made kissing noises and faces, and I copied her. Jade rolled her eyes.

"Freaks," she said, grabbing a soda. But she smiled, too, just a little. I saw it. I swear.

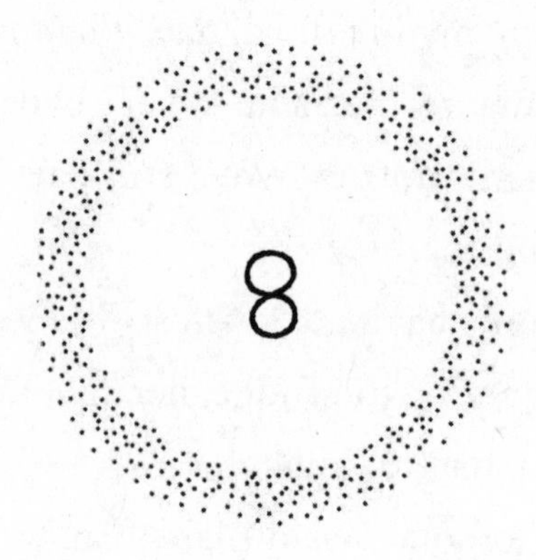

AUGUST, PRESENT DAY

Twelve years old

"I'm sorry, *what*?" I asked. "You have a Star-Gazer Twelve? And you think it's buried at the Moose Junction Library?"

Simone and Dr. Lacamoire glanced at each other.

"Underground," I clarified.

"That is what the word *buried* means, yes," said Dr. Lacamoire smoothly.

"I told you," snapped Simone. "I told you this was a waste of our time." She looked back at me. "I'm sorry, Abby. We shouldn't have bothered you."

"It's just—it sounds kind of . . . you know. Hard to believe," I said. "A time capsule? And why would there be a Star-Gazer Twelve in it? How did it *get* there?"

Dr. Lacamoire shook his head. "That's the wrong question. The question is, how are we going to get it *out*?"

"We?" I asked.

"Yes. You have to help. You're friendly with the librarian. You know the lay of the land. I can't just take a bulldozer to the place, as much as I'd like to," he said. "I need someone familiar with the library to help me figure out where exactly it's buried on the library grounds, and then procure it while I'm otherwise occupied. They would never expect some local child to have dug the thing up."

I shook my head. "First of all, I'm not even sure there *is* a time capsule."

"Show her!" Dr. Lacamoire barked at Simone. She rolled her eyes but pulled a piece of paper off the mantel and handed it to me. It was a black-and-white photo of a group of people in City Hall. I even recognized some of them. Joe Kitt from the hardware store still had that same denim shirt, but his hair was blond instead of its current gray. Miss Mae. My grandmother! My own grandma, smiling wide. In front of them was a table full of stuff, from books to a creepy-looking doll to a baseball.

And circled in red, the Star-Gazer Twelve. One of the best telescopes in the world.

Preserving Time, the headline read. The caption of the photo: *Citizens of Moose Junction buried a time capsule outside the Moose Junction Public Library this weekend to preserve what life was like in the small resort town in 2000.*

"There," said Dr. Lacamoire confidently. "Proof. That article came from *Waukegan Weekly*. I printed it from the archives. I thought for sure there would be some sort of detail about *where* the thing was, but of course, this was probably Jim Bob Smith, the Reporter. Not exactly an *investigator*. They should have higher standards."

Yes, because there was so often breaking news here in the Northwoods. The last time Moose Junction had made the *Waukegan Weekly* was when an albino deer had been spotted.

"But if it's yours, how did it wind up in the time capsule?" I asked again.

Simone's eyes shot toward Dr. Lacamoire. His entire face turned stony. I had clearly tiptoed onto some forbidden land.

"Not by any fault of mine, I assure you," he said flatly. "The telescope was stolen. I've been searching for it for years, and it was recently revealed to me . . . No, no, Abigail, don't ask how! These are the *wrong questions*. That the thief buried it in this time capsule is what we should be focusing on. The telescope is mine. I want it back. And you're the only one who can help me."

I just stared at him. An MIT professor with one of the most-viewed TED Talks on YouTube, begging me for help.

"Why can't we just *ask* someone where exactly on the grounds it's buried?" I said. "All of these people were there. Someone should know."

"Because it might seem a *tad* suspicious when a week later, it turns out the thing was dug up," said Simone.

"But how would they even know it was taken?" I asked.

"This isn't some tiny thing. It's large. We'd have to dig a significant hole. The fresh mound of dirt wouldn't tip people off?" said Simone pointedly.

"I mean . . . I doubt it. It's not like we have a shortage of dirt around here," I said.

"We can't take chances," said Dr. Lacamoire firmly. "We need to know exactly where the capsule is buried—"

"*And* we need to make sure we don't get in trouble for digging it up," Simone finished for him. "So. Our best shot is metal detectors. They sell them at the hardware place in town. We need to go to the library one night and figure out where exactly the thing is buried, and then you'd need to return another night to dig it up."

"It's going to be tricky," said Dr. Lacamoire. "You'll have to go at a time when I'm somewhere else, for a solid alibi, but also during hours when nobody in town would be driving past."

I knew the perfect time. But I had a question first.

"So, what's in it for me?" I asked.

Simone looked surprised, but Dr. Lacamoire simply looked at me.

"I'm just saying," I continued. "This is probably illegal. If nothing else, I'd get the grounding of my life if I got busted. So what are you planning on doing for me?"

"It seems as if you have something in mind," said Dr. Lacamoire.

I did.

"Listen, Abigail," Dr. Lacamoire started.

"Abby."

"This telescope was the most important item I owned," he said, his voice quiet. "It means everything to me. I will do anything—*anything*—to get it back. I'll give you whatever you want. But I am begging you to help me."

Maybe I could help two people at once.

"I need an introduction," I said.

"Done," said Dr. Lacamoire instantly. But Simone held a hand up.

"Wait a second. God, Leo. To who?" She seemed suspicious.

"To your book editor," I said.

That surprised both of them.

"*Joanna?*" asked Simone. "What on earth for?"

So that she could turn *Planet Pirates* into a real book that went to real libraries.

So that Blair and I could be best friends again.

So that I could save my sister.

She'd forget all about ballet if we were famous comic book writers. I could fix it. I could fix it all. Even my dad knew how important "that comic thing" was to Blair. Her smile after the Joffrey meltdown, when I passed *Planet Pirates* back to her—it reminded me that anything was possible. But I needed Joanna Creech's help to do it.

This was my only chance. When I'd googled Dr. Lacamoire, Joanna's name had come up over and over again. They'd been working together for years. She wasn't any old editor—she was one of the best. She had edited almost one hundred other books, and a bunch had gone on to be *New York Times* bestsellers. She had a fancy office in a real skyscraper. Even her picture made me want to work with her. She had a tight bun, dangly earrings, and her eyes seemed to say *I got this.*

She probably got eighty emails a day from aspiring writers who thought they'd written the next Harry Potter. Billions of people think they're good enough to have books in Barnes & Noble. But I wasn't dumb, no matter what Jade thought. I knew I needed someone to knock on her door for me first.

"Don't say another word," said Dr. Lacamoire, holding up a hand. "It's done."

"But, *Leo—*"

"Simone, for heaven's sake, Jo is one phone call away. It's an easy trade-off for the return of my telescope."

Simone stared at me, eyebrows narrowed. She didn't trust me. Fine. Maybe she shouldn't.

I never said I was perfect. That was Blair.

"Then I know how to help," I said. "The eclipse."

It would be hard to pull off. Nearly impossible, really. Dad and I had been talking about the eclipse ever since it had been announced. We'd ordered our glasses, made plans, and counted down the days. Everyone was expecting me to be at the viewing party. But the whole town would be distracted, and Dr. Lacamoire could easily be visible. While residents and tourists alike were focused on the day becoming night, I would dig up the time capsule and retrieve the Star-Gazer Twelve.

"That could be perfect," he mused. "No one will be at the library then?"

"No way. This eclipse is the biggest thing that's ever happened here. *Everyone* will be on Main Street," I assured him.

"Will that be enough time?" asked Simone. "Eclipses aren't long. A couple of minutes, tops."

"Sure. But people will be on Main Street all day. There's a big viewing party. Trust me, nobody's going to be at the library. I doubt Harriet will even open it up that day. Especially if I go digging when the eclipse is taking place. It would take me, like, thirty minutes. Tops."

Simone nodded thoughtfully. "It could work."

"It *has* to work," Dr. Lacamoire reminded her.

"It might be hard for me to sneak away from my dad," I admitted. "But I can do it. You'll get your telescope. I'll get my introduction."

"It sounds to me like we have a deal, Abigail," said Dr. Lacamoire smoothly.

"It's *Abby*, Dr. Lacamoire."

"Call me Leo."

So the plan was in motion. When I said yes, and so

did he, we kicked off an adventure that we couldn't have possibly guessed would end the way it did. I had my reasons, and Dr. Leo Lacamoire had his, and Simone even had hers. But together, we had a shared mission. One that involved lying and deceit and probable disaster, sure, but a mission nonetheless.

"Mom?" I went into the office the next day, where my mother was going over some spreadsheets. "Do you have a sec?"

"Sure thing, sweets. Just trying to get a few last-minute things in order. Can you believe the eclipse is in eight days? We have three new renters this week. One cabin was booked by the *New York Times*!"

"That's awesome," I said. I plopped down in the other office chair and spun around in it.

"So what's on your mind?" She didn't take her eyes off the spreadsheets.

I had to play this the right way. I thought about my words carefully.

"Someone was looking at the *Waukegan Weekly* archives at the library last week for a school project, and I saw a picture of Grandma," I said.

"In the newspaper? *Your* grandma?" Now Mom

looked up, surprised. "That's funny. For what?"

"A time capsule," I said. "It was just random."

Okay, Leo had told me not to ask anyone. But I didn't think the thing getting dug up would make national headlines. I mean, the eclipse was all anyone could think about. Main Street was decorated with twinkly lights—which would of course be turned off for the eclipse—and cutouts of shooting stars were in all the store windows. There were already news vans parked outside Hank's Hardware and More, too. Besides, if I put the dirt right back, it might not even be noticeable. And if Mom did hear about it, chances of her suspecting me were low. I didn't do things like sneak around and dig up secret time capsules. At least, she didn't think I did.

And if she asked, I'd lie. I was getting better at it.

I wished I could just call my grandma about the capsule, but she had died when I was in kindergarten. I didn't remember her much, just flashes of pie crust being spread across a plate and old hymns she'd always hum. There was a framed photo of her on one of our bookshelves, and I knew Mom still went to the cemetery in Milwaukee on her birthday every year. We had an afghan she'd knitted folded over the living room couch, and sometimes, I'd bury my face in it and inhale deeply.

But it had been washed a thousand times; you couldn't smell her anymore.

"Really? Never heard about that. When was it?"

"The year 2000," I said.

"Well, that explains it. That was the year your dad and I were gallivanting around Europe like a couple of college kids," chuckled Mom. "Our last big adventure pre-Blair. We were gone, what, eight months? We probably missed the whole thing."

I nodded. "So, you don't know anything about it?"

"I don't. That's pretty cool, though. Can I see the picture?"

"I didn't print it. I will next time I go to the library," I said.

"Thanks. What are you up to today? It's gorgeous out, finally. I thought that rain would never end. You should see if Sophie and Lex want to go out on the paddleboards."

I shrugged.

"Everything okay there, Abigail? You girls in a fight or something?"

"No," I said annoyed. "They're just busy." Busy having the best summer ever, from the look of their Instagrams.

"Okay. Sure," Mom said hesitantly. "I saw Vanessa at Coontail's on Wednesday, and she said Sophie was missing you." Sophie's mom. Oh, she was, huh? Did she break her fingers taking too many selfies with Lex and lose her ability to send a text message? Did she fall and get amnesia?

"Whatever," I grumbled. "I'm gonna go swim or something."

I got up to leave, but she stopped me.

"Abby? We're going back to see Blair tomorrow. I know you don't want to go, but we're doing a family therapy session. Jade is coming, too. I want us to all be on the same page when she comes home. She's doing so much better, sweets. It would mean a lot to me if you would come."

My parents would be out of town? Sounded like a great time to get metal detectors.

And it sounded like a great time to *not* see Blair. What would we even talk about? What was there to say?

"Just think about it," Mom said, her voice pleading. "She misses you, Abby. She asks about you every time I talk to her. I think she feels bad that you saw . . . the cupcake thing."

"I'll think about it," I said. But Mom just looked away sadly. Remember what I said: sometimes, I'm a liar.

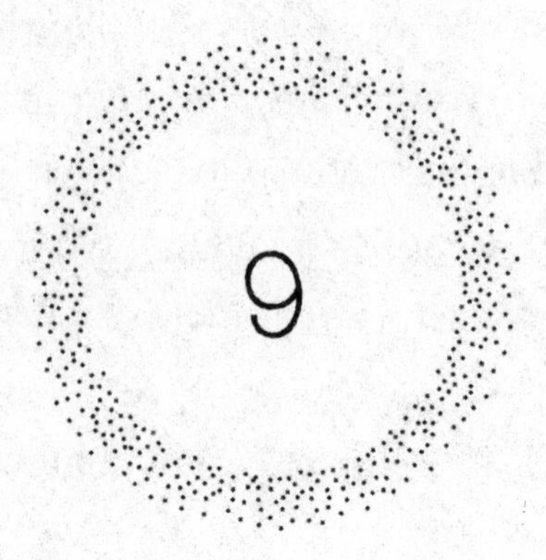

AUGUST, PRESENT DAY

Twelve years old

We had a game plan.

I'd always thought I wanted to be an astronomer when I grew up. MIT, NASA, spending my nights looking up at the sky. But I thought the strategy I had formulated for Operation Star-Gazer Twelve Retrieval was pretty good. Maybe I should consider a career as a spy.

Here's how it would go down:

Day: August 25.

Time: 2:12 p.m.

The eclipse, the eclipse, the eclipse: the entire town consumed, waiting for those few magical minutes. Dr.

Leo Lacamoire had responsibilities. He was going to be interviewed by CNN on what an eclipse was and why the day was going dark. I would ditch my dad and high-tail it to the library on my bike just before the moon hid the sun. I'd dig up the time capsule with a shovel I'd hide the night before, retrieve the telescope, and leave it in the kitchen of Eagle's Nest. Then I'd race back to Main Street, nobody the wiser.

Okay, there were a few flaws.

Maybe more than a few. In fact, the more time passed, the dumber the whole thing seemed.

For starters, my dad. How was I supposed to sneak away from him? We'd been talking about the eclipse for months. It was Our Thing—the sky—and I was supposed to just miss it?

Then there was the part where I was supposed to somehow lug around a telescope on my bike. I'd had the same one since I was seven. It had Thomas the Tank Engine stickers on it, for cripes' sake. It wasn't exactly a *truck*—telescopes are heavy.

And what about timing? The eclipse was supposed to last about two minutes. I had told Leo it would take me thirty. But I was kinda doubtful that I could dig a deep hole and haul out an enormous box in that amount of time, let alone bike the thing back to Eagle's Nest.

So it wasn't *perfect*. But Dad would hopefully be distracted, yapping with other people in town, and he'd forgive me, eventually, for disappearing. As for the bike issue, well, I could always balance big stuff on my handlebars. If they could hold Sophie, they could hold a telescope. Even if it took longer than expected, the library wasn't on Main Street—it was a mile and a half away, off Uselman. Nobody would be driving around. If anyone, by chance, *did* see me with a box, I'd say it was some delivery for my parents. And soon enough, Dr. Lacamoire and Simone would be long gone, taking the evidence with them.

There was still another problem, a Big Glaring Issue that was hard to tackle. We knew the time capsule was buried in front of the library where everyone posed for that picture. We just didn't know *where*. For that, as mentioned before, we'd need metal detectors. And for *that*, we'd need a hardware store.

"I am *not* stealing from Joe," I said firmly.

I was sitting in the living room of Eagle's Nest. Simone was wearing a swimsuit with a cover-up, and Leo had on that white stuff old people wear on their nose so they don't get sunburned.

"Joe? You mean Hank?" asked Simone.

"Joe owns Hank's Hardware and More. Hank was his grandpa's cat or something," I said. "And he's really nice."

"The cat or Joe?" asked Simone.

"I'm *not* stealing from him!"

"Nobody's asking you to *steal.* You're being very dramatic," said Leo, waving a hand. "We're *paying* for the metal detectors, for heaven's sake. I would never shoplift. We're just purchasing them after hours."

"When there isn't anyone there. And the door is locked," I said.

"You're not thinking clearly, Abby!" said Leo, annoyed. "Metal detectors? Then a dug-up time capsule? *Hello?* We'll be prime suspects."

"I don't get it," I said, shaking my head. "You're acting like Moose Junction is going to get its entire police force on this. And if they do, it's Officer J.J. He does the presentations about smoking at our school. His main job is getting cats out of trees. He's not exactly Sherlock Holmes."

"We can't be too careful," said Leo. "We'll leave the money right on the counter. Tell me you don't know where John keeps the keys."

"*Joe.*" And of course I did. They were under the mat,

though he probably didn't even lock the doors. There hadn't been a real crime in Moose Junction since some college kids vacationing here let a deer loose in Coontail's.

"I'll buy them," I said. "I'll tell him it's for . . . a school project." Mr. Linn flashed in my head: *O, what a tangled web we weave when first we practice to deceive!* Some old dead guy had said that once, and Mr. Linn repeated it whenever someone claimed their dog ate their homework. It's better to be honest, he'd said, and face the consequences.

Well. Easy for him to say. He was an English teacher. His life wasn't that complicated.

"In August," Simone pointed out.

"Summer school! Look, digging up the time capsule won't send us to jail. But breaking into a hardware store might," I said. "Besides, security cameras? Hello?"

They both looked stumped at that, even though I highly doubted Joe had cameras in the store. He could build a bench or fix a roof but he still needed help sending text messages. He didn't even take credit cards.

"Fine," said Simone. "I say we go for Abby's plan. I just don't want them pinning this on Leo."

"Done," I said.

Leo handed over some cash, a few crisp bills that were larger than any I'd ever held in my life.

"Good luck, stargazer," said Simone.

The two of them headed out back toward the dock, talking about some TV appearance Leo had booked for the fall. They had plans to take a boat out, which made me nervous. Leo said if he could find new planets he could probably operate a speedboat, but they weren't really the same skill set. Whatever. Mom and Dad's problem, not mine.

I was learning some things about Leo, more than you could find in a Google search. For starters, he was a person with secrets. That was okay by me; everyone has pieces of their life they don't want to talk about. Sometimes at sleepovers Lex cried a little in the middle of the night and I'd never even asked her why. I have plenty of stuff I wouldn't broadcast on a billboard. But Leo had never mentioned any family or friends besides Simone. He said he was "married to work," whatever that meant.

He could also zone out in the middle of conversations. Earlier, when we'd been plotting our time capsule mission, Simone was going on and on about the exact timing of the eclipse. When we asked Leo his thoughts, he blinked as if he hadn't even been in the room. He'd been thinking about the galaxy, he said. What about it, I'm not sure any of us knew.

Mom had actually become buddies with Simone. I would look outside sometimes and see the two of them chatting on the front porch of Eagle's Nest, Mom usually talking and Simone nodding, occasionally bursting into laughter. I could see Mom chuckling and giving off "mm-hmms" while Simone ranted about Leo's obsession with his coffee being a certain temperature, and Mom in return would go off about the reporters from Chicago who kept complaining about the sometimes-unreliable Wi-Fi. The other night, they'd even gone to the Green Lantern together. I'd spied on Leo through my telescope. He'd been busy with his own stars, testing out his different telescopes in the observatory. I couldn't help but wonder how on earth the Star-Gazer Twelve had slipped from his grasp and wound up buried. How could you let something like that go?

I rode my bike into town. I'd obviously opted not to go to Harvest Hills. I couldn't believe Jade was going, but she'd gotten someone to take her shift at the theater and everything. Mom asked me again in the morning but I'd said I had a headache. Sitting around pretending Blair was going to come home and everything would be perfect felt like a waste of time. I didn't want to see her, sad and skinny, in a visitors' area with a bunch of sick people. Blair belonged in a place where she could be dancing or drawing, under a spotlight with all eyes on her. Not in a place with depressed-looking brochures. On the Harvest Hills website, they had a huge picture of a girl with long blond hair and sad eyes looking out a window. It didn't exactly make you want to spend a day there.

Once upon a time, Blair had been my favorite person in the world. But that was before Anna Rexia blindfolded her and kept her prisoner. Now, just thinking about her made my throat start to pinch shut. It was a lot easier to pretend Jade was my only sister, as terrible as I know that sounds.

You can judge me all you want. *You* live with someone who's afraid of a cupcake and tell me how it feels. *You* let your best friend be kidnapped by a monster and act like everything's fine. Family, love, support, blah blah blah—more brochure words. The truth is, sometimes you just want to eat a family dinner without someone bursting into tears.

I walked into Hank's Hardware and More, waving to Joe, and found the metal detectors. Man, those things were expensive! I grabbed three and went up to the counter, playing it cool.

"Hey, Abby," said Joe. "Going treasure hunting?"

"Extra credit project. Summer school," I said. Hey, I was getting good at this. Apparently lying was like ballet: the more you practiced, the more graceful you became.

"Where are you taking these things? The shore?"

"Yup," I said, nodding. I should really do that, I thought. Snap an Instagram. Make it look extra convincing. Not that Joe was perusing social media.

"You, Sophie, and Lex working together?"

"What?"

"Three of 'em," he said as he rang them up.

"Oh. Yup. Group project." Of course, now I had to be paranoid that he was going to run into them and ask them how the metal detectors were working. Lies—they grew and grew. You could drop a seed by accident and find yourself with a field full of weeds.

"Hey, by the way, how's Blair? Georgia wanted me to ask." Joe's wife loved Blair. She even drove to Milwaukee once to see her in *The Nutcracker*. But really, everyone loved Blair. I could hardly walk down the street without someone asking about her.

"She's good," I said, forcing a smile. As if I knew.

I hadn't seen her in months. I knew about as much as Georgia did.

"Good to hear."

The next phase of the plan was simple: meet at the library at midnight. Except for the very obvious facts that I shared a bedroom, it was on the second floor, and Obi was the world's lightest sleeper, of course.

My family came home late that evening. The sky was clear and I had been up in the attic, still looking for Scorpius. As usual, everyone was exhausted, but maybe a little happy, too. Mom and Dad were, at least. Jade seemed ticked off.

"Who peed in your Cocoa Puffs?" I asked her when she slammed our bedroom door.

"Shut up," she said. "I just spent, like, all day talking about my feelings. I need to take a shower or something. Get all the sap-crap off of me."

"I don't know why you even went," I said.

"I'm surprised you *didn't* go," she said. "Saint Abby didn't want to do exactly what Mom asked her?"

I glared at her and rolled over. Hopefully, she'd fall asleep early. Obi may wake up at the drop of a hat, but Jade could usually sleep through just about anything.

"It wasn't so bad," she said from her bed, staring up at her ceiling. "I mean. I told Blair what I thought. About how messed up she had been last year. And how I wanted her to be okay before she came home."

I squeezed my eyes shut. *Stop, stop, stop.* I wanted to hear everything and nothing at the same time. I wanted every detail and total silence. I wanted Blair to be perfect and Blair to not exist. I wanted a crack to open up in the Earth, swallow me whole, and spit me back up into the stars. I wanted to ride a rocket to the moon and start a colony there where Anna Rexia could never find me.

"Maybe next time you'll come. Or not. Whatever. She's coming home in nine days; did you know that?" said Jade.

Nine days. Nine days until Blair would be back, counting calories and causing Mom to get worried eyes. The mood in the house would return to being a thunderstorm. Dr. Leo Lacamoire and his Star-Gazer Twelve would be headed to Massachusetts.

"I'm tired," I said, reaching over and turning out my light. "Let's go to sleep."

While I waited for Jade to start snoring, I thought about the time capsule. All those memories, stuffed in one place. What would I put in my own time capsule?

The first draft of *Planet Pirates*.

Dolphy, my creatively named stuffed dolphin that I still slept with every night.

Honey Nut Cheerios, which I ate for breakfast every single morning.

One of Obi's chew toys.

Maybe some pictures, too. Of Obi when he was a puppy and we brought him home from the pound looking like a fluffy little snowball. My mom in her garden with those crazy polka-dot gloves she loved. The one of the five of us picking out a Christmas tree that my mom kept in the office. I had on such a puffy coat you couldn't even see my face, but my sisters looked so happy. Pictures are kind of like stars. When you see a star, you're really glimpsing light from something that died, like, a bajillion years ago. But the glow is still there, even if the star isn't.

It seemed nice—the idea of capturing a moment just as it was. Maybe that was why Sophie and Lex felt the need to post every single thing they did on their iPhones. I thought of the photo from the newspaper. Those poor people from twenty years ago didn't know about all the bad stuff that would happen afterward, all the sad things taking place in the world. Mom didn't even like to have the TV on because there was always some serious-looking newscaster talking about bombs or wars or car crashes. When Moose Junction residents put together their time capsule, it was like they were taking a picture of a time everything was perfect. What came next was just a big empty slate—until real life set in, taking over.

I suddenly felt bad about uncovering the time capsule. Didn't those people, like my own grandma, deserve to leave their stuff buried in a nice safe box? Weren't some things better left underground?

Jade let out a particularly loud snore and I knew the coast was clear. The TV had been turned off in Mom and Dad's room, too; they usually went to sleep early.

I got out of bed as quietly as possible and pulled on a black sweatshirt of Jade's that I had grabbed from her closet. I tiptoed down the stairs, past a sleeping Norwegian elkhound, and out the door.

The bike ride to the library wasn't far, but it was chilly out. By the time I showed up, Simone and Leo were already walking around with their detectors.

"You look like a bank robber," said Simone.

"You look like a neon sign," I shot back. She had on a bright purple jacket you could see from a million miles away. Leo was in an MIT sweatshirt, which was at least a darker gray.

"Just get to looking, stargazer," she said, shoving the third metal detector into my hand.

We split up and walked around the grounds to cover our bases. Just because the photo was taken out front of the library didn't mean the capsule was actually buried there. Simone went to the side of the building, and Leo and I stayed out front, walking slowly with our metal detectors. I kept peering down the street. I had talked a big talk earlier, but this *wasn't* illegal, was it? Officer J.J. couldn't haul us off to jail? Was a library public property? I couldn't help stealing glances up at the sky, too. There were so many stars out, it felt like we were in a painting. The Big Dipper danced across the sky, so easy to find, even without a telescope. No matter what craziness was happening down here on Earth, those stars just kept doing their thing.

"So," said Dr. Lacamoire. "You want to write a book?"

"What?" My breath came out in a puff of air.

"Joanna," he said. "Why else would you want to meet her?"

I was glad he couldn't see how awkward I looked. Some people will just tell anyone who will listen what their dreams are. Hand them a megaphone and they'll go to town. Like Jade's friend Cassidee who's always blabbing about how the second she turns eighteen she's moving to Los Angeles and becoming an actress. Guess what? If it doesn't happen because, hello, *tons* of people want to be on TV, everyone will be embarrassed for her. If you *really* want something, you shouldn't tell the world about it. Then when it all goes to crap, the only person who thinks you're stupid is you.

Blair. The Joffrey. All those disappointed looks, all those questions about New York? She shouldn't have let herself dream. She shouldn't have—

"Guys!" hissed Simone. "I've got something!"

We dashed to the side corner of the property where Simone was standing. She waved us over hurriedly. Her detector was going *nuts*.

"We've got it," said Leo excitedly. "This has to be the capsule!"

Simone grinned. "Finally."

"Why don't we just dig it up now and be done with it?" said Leo. "We're so close." He squatted down and held a hand to the grass, as if he could reach through the Earth and snatch up his telescope. More than the telescope. He was desperate to find—

No! We aren't there yet. We're at the part of the story where he's frantic and fraught over the Star-Gazer Twelve. Where I'm making promises I'm not sure I can keep.

"We can't," I said. "Too risky." As if to prove my point, a lone car rumbled by. We all jumped about a foot.

"Soon," said Simone, putting her hand on Leo's shoulder. "You'll have it back soon. Right, Abby?"

I swallowed. To dig up that time capsule would be a lie—to Harriet, to all the people who had buried it.

But I could save Blair. Or, at least, Joanna Creech could. There wouldn't be any pretending. We could send Anna Rexia away for good, waving as she drove down the street and out of our lives.

I nodded.

"Soon."

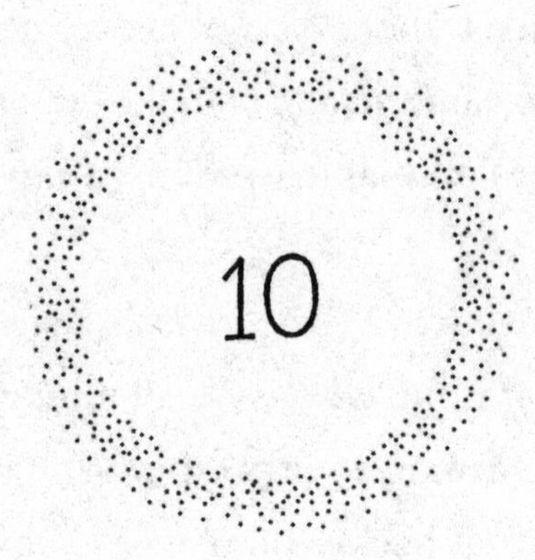

AUGUST, TWO YEARS AGO

Ten years old

Two years before we set out with metal detectors to find hidden things, Dr. Leo Lacamoire was on a mission to repair something that had been broken. He wasn't looking for a telescope; he was looking for a person, and he was desperate to find her. Two years ago, the Star-Gazer Twelve was safe underground, but he did not know that yet.

Two years ago, I didn't know who Dr. Leo Lacamoire was. I was about to enter the sixth grade. Middle school, where you didn't get recess and had to switch classrooms for different subjects. Sophie, Lex, and I had decorated our binders with lyrics we liked and photographs of the three of us. Lex had a picture of Harry Styles without his shirt on glued to her science one, which my mom would never let me do.

Blair was going to be a junior in high school, but she didn't want to go. She wanted to be tutored.

"Aleksander says that it's time I start taking my career seriously. If I want to do ballet as a profession, I can't be wasting my time learning about geometry," Blair complained.

We were at dinner, eating baked chicken. We'd all been trying to eat healthier since Mom had seen some documentary about the horror of trans fats. The night before, Dad had snuck the three of us out to get milkshakes, making us swear up and down we wouldn't tell her. Blair wouldn't order one, though; she said junk food slowed her down at ballet. She thought it was why she didn't get the lead in *Swan Lake* this year even though she had done so well in *Coppélia*. The girl who had gotten the part Blair wanted was so skinny you could have broken her in half. I didn't think it was pretty at all, but when I told Blair that, she just rolled her eyes, which made her look like Jade. Blair was always asking Mom if she could help cook, now—I heard them arguing about butter and whether or not Greek yogurt could really match up to sour cream.

"I don't know, Blair," said Mom. "You'd miss out on so much. Don't you want to be a normal kid for just a little bit longer?"

"What do colleges think of homeschooling?" asked Dad, pointing his fork at her. "What would this do to your transcripts?"

"You guys. I'm not *trying* to be a normal kid! I'm trying to follow my *dreams*, here."

"I say if she wants to be a homeschool freak, let her," said Jade. "Then we wouldn't have to go to the same school." Jade was a freshman, thinking she was all that, wearing more makeup than she was supposed to and talking back to Mom and Dad. She was starting to get really annoying. Why did she have to say things like that? It was like she had forgotten that we had ever been best friends. If she was snarky enough, maybe she thought we'd all just poof into thin air.

I picked at my brussels sprouts. Why do parents even make brussels sprouts? Does anyone in the entire world like them? I mean, I know they're healthy, but man, at what cost?

"Dad, you're thinking too small," said Blair. "Transcripts? I don't care about transcripts. I'm not trying to go to Yale. I'm trying to get accepted into a professional company."

"But your grades are so high," said Dad, looking a little crushed. Mom cared about your friends, your social life, your dental hygiene, and your general happiness. Dad cared what your report card said. "You won the science fair that time, remember? With the lava lamp . . ."

"In fifth grade," said Blair flatly. "Do you realize how much these girls who get hired practice? Seven, eight hours a day! They aren't making homemade lava lamps!"

They said they'd think about it. I already knew what would happen. Blair could be persistent when she wanted to be. Whether it was a custom-made tutu or a summer dance camp in Chicago, what she begged for, she usually got. She had Dreams. A Passion. She was Going Places. We were just standing in her shadow. Jade, with her eyeliner obsession and bad attitude, could try all she wanted to get out, but I was just fine in the shade.

Sure enough, a few weeks later, Jade and I headed off on the bus while Blair got driven by my mom to Milwaukee every day. She had dance for seven hours and would then come home and race through math workbooks, checking all the right boxes to make sure she kept our parents happy. But she was no longer Blair who danced. She was a dancer named Blair. And it felt different.

Other times, she felt like the same old Blair. That Halloween, she somehow convinced Jade to be the third Sanderson sister from *Hocus Pocus*, and we won the costume contest at Town Hall. I still have the picture of us leaning over a cauldron, crazy-eyed and wild-haired. That picture would probably go in my time capsule, too.

There were things that *had* changed. Blair had always been stressed out about stuff, especially when it came to dance, but she started to take it to a whole new level. I'd see her light on in the middle of the night and hear her stretching, running in place, practicing her turns. When we went shopping for new Christmas dresses that year, Blair had suddenly started crying in the dressing room and wouldn't tell anyone why. Mom had rubbed her back and talked to her in a quiet voice, just handing over her credit card to Jade and telling us to buy whatever and meet them in the car.

Blair was working a ton on *Planet Pirates*, too, constantly drawing on her way to and from the ballet studio. It seemed like art was the only thing that calmed her down after dance got her all worked up. If she got done with homework after I'd gone to bed, I'd wake up to her drawings shoved under my door, a sticky note on top. *What happens next?* it read.

None of us knew. That was the problem. If we had seen what was coming barreling down the road, we would have stopped it. But we were like those poor suckers burying their memories underground, and like Dr. Leo Lacamoire as things slipped out of his grasp. We had no idea of what was to come.

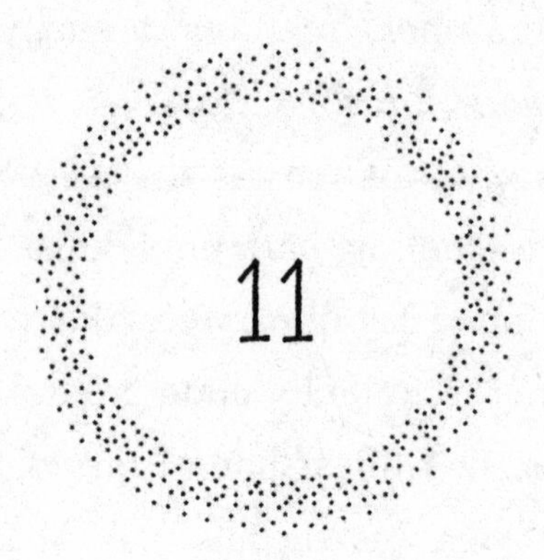

11

AUGUST, PRESENT DAY

Twelve years old

The morning after my midnight escapade, Mom and Dad dragged Jade and me to church, same as every Sunday. Usually I don't mind Mass that much, but it was *hot*, and St. Rita's didn't have air-conditioning. Whenever anyone complains, Father Peter Patrick reminds them of Jesus living in a desert for forty days with no food or water, and everyone shuts up real fast. But it's hard to listen to some Big Important Message when you're sweating through your dress. Jade was trying to text, but Dad took her phone.

Father Peter Patrick was going on and on about perseverance in the face of trials. I thought about what trials I'd been through. The time trials at school when we had to run around the track and I was usually the last one to finish. But I knew that wasn't what he meant. He meant stuff like Sophie and Lex dumping me, or losing Blair, or figuring out what to do about this time capsule.

Something about what he was saying got to Mom. She talked to Father Peter Patrick for a few minutes after church, and when we got home, she announced that she was cleaning out Blair's room.

"It's time for a fresh start," she said. "A reset."

"You're just gonna go in the Sugar Plum Fairy's room and dig through her stuff?" asked Jade.

"She asked me to," said Mom. It was only six days until the eclipse, seven until Blair was supposed to come home. "She said dance made her think bad thoughts, and she wanted anything related to it out of there. She even asked me if I could paint. It's about a billion degrees outside, but I'm in the mood."

"I'll help," said Jade, which surprised me.

"Aren't you going to go floating or something?" I asked her.

"God, do you think I'm incapable of doing anything nice?" snapped Jade. "Besides, it's too hot to be outside. Even on the water."

"You better be praying with that language, Jade Marie. But I appreciate the extra set of hands. You in, Abigail? Your dad has to go fix the water heater over at Heron."

I shrugged. Something about it felt wrong. I went downstairs and made myself a peanut butter and jelly sandwich, scrolling through Sophie's Instagram account while I ate. She'd perfected the selfie. We used to make fun of girls for pictures like that; zoomed-in squares of their face where they were trying to look serious but smile with their eyes. She had on a ton of mascara. Her mom hadn't even let her wear makeup to school last year.

Laughter.

I glanced upstairs. Mom and Jade were laughing; *howling*, like they were watching the funniest movie in the world. What could be so hilarious about digging through a treasure trove of all the things we'd lost?

I took the steps to our floor and saw them—Mom and Jade, lying on Blair's bed, flipping through a photo album. It was chaos around them. There was a pile of tutus haphazardly thrown together in one corner, and papers all over Blair's desk. Some of her old school workbooks were stacked to the side with a pencil cup she had made in third grade. Everything that had been under her bed was dragged out. A handful of paint swatches was lying on the ground, abandoned. Poor Misty Copeland was folded in half.

"Oh, Abigail," said Mom, gasping between her giggles. Jade was wiping away tears. "Get in here. This is too much."

Jade scooted over and I plopped next to her on the bed. Mom held out the album and showed me. The three of us as the Sanderson sisters, making ridiculous faces. Blair even had fake teeth.

"You girls!" said Mom. "That was such a fun year. Even though Jade threw up all of her candy the next morning."

"Don't remind me. Show her the one with the newspaper," said Jade, barely able to speak from laughing. Mom flipped the page, and there was toddler Blair, making a ridiculous face, butt naked, with a newspaper draped over her head.

"That face!" cried Mom. Jade cracked up. They paged through more photos, some I remembered, some I didn't.

Click. Blair, Jade, and me, in sparkly swimsuits, running through a sprinkler.

Click. Obi as a puppy, licking Blair's face.

Click. Blair after one of her first recitals, in way too much makeup, sticking her tongue out and crossing her eyes. Jade next to her, pulling her nose up like a pig.

Mom and Jade laughed and laughed, but I wanted to scream.

This was just light from stars that had already died.

This Blair—putting newspapers on her head, playing with Obi, being silly—she was gone. Gone in a pile of calories and toe shoes and therapy appointments, of lies and deceit and tears. We see those stars, and we pretend they're there, but they're *not.*

I slammed the photo book shut and left, abandoning Mom and Jade silent behind me. I went into my room and closed the door, not even opening it for Obi's scratches.

"Abigail?" Mom asked an hour later, poking her head in. "You okay in there?"

No. I felt like I couldn't breathe. Why was I the only one who could see the truth? They all still had that prom night feeling, like Blair could magically go backward. That hope kept knocking on their doors. I had lit mine on fire. It was gone, as gone as those stars, as gone as my sister and her dreams.

Only I could bring them back. With Dr. Leo Lacamoire's help.

✲ ✲ ✲

That night, there was a knock on our front door. It was Simone, inviting me to Leo's observatory. The stars were particularly bright tonight, she told my mom. They were really something.

I wanted to ask my dad along—he would have loved those telescopes. But Simone was giving me a Look, a we-have-something-to-discuss Look, and Dad was at the Green Lantern with Harrison anyway, so I hurried up to my room to grab Jade's work sweatshirt.

As I was walking back downstairs, I peeked into Blair's room. So much of her stuff was gone, tucked neatly into boxes that would be placed into storage. Mom was nothing if not organized. Some of the posters were gone; Princess Leia and Hermione Granger still stared down from her walls, but Misty Copeland had disappeared without a trace. So had her certificates from ballet summer intensives and a few newspaper articles about her dance company that Mom had framed. Everything she had worked so hard for now had to be hidden, tucked away where no one could find them.

Simone and I walked right past Eagle's Nest.

"Where are we going?" I asked.

"Leo wants to set up a scope down by the shore, in this little cutout area. Zero lights. Also seems like a good place to go over the plan," said Simone. "It really is a nice night." She was right; it was so warm I really didn't even need the sweatshirt. Once the sun had vanished, the intense heat had gone away, and we were left with the perfect temperature for a summer night. The stars were sprinkled around the sky, fireflies were sputtering across the lake, and you could hear the loons calling. It felt like we were in a postcard for northern Wisconsin.

We walked a little farther in silence.

"Ran into your mom earlier this afternoon at the hardware store," said Simone.

"I thought you were afraid of being caught in the hardware store," I said.

"I had to get some Sharpies. Leo's very particular about his writing utensils. But *anyway*. I saw your mom buying paint. She said she was putting a new coat on your sister's room."

I froze. I hadn't said a word about my sisters—either of them—to Leo or Simone. Maybe for once I didn't want to be Blair McCourt's little sister. Especially now, when everyone in town knew her as the girl who flipped out over a cupcake. Sophie and Lex had probably told every single one of our friends from school, even. *Abby's big sister lost her mind over dessert.*

"She told me Blair's spending the summer in a treatment facility. That she has an eating disorder," said Simone hesitantly. "You didn't tell me that. Or that you even had another sister."

I scowled. "I barely *know* you."

"You know me well enough to help us out, stargazer."

"Because I need an introduction to Joanna Creech. Not because I'm nice."

That made Simone chuckle.

"Yeah, well, he wants you to do more. He wants you to double-check that the spot we found is really where it's buried. By asking that librarian. The big one?"

"Her name is Harriet," I mumbled.

"Yeah. See if she knows anything. Leo's paranoid. Starting to doubt himself." She rubbed her hands on her arms. It was getting kind of chilly.

"I just don't get what a twelve-year-old needs to talk to a book editor for," Simone continued.

"*I* just don't get how this treasured telescope wound up in a time capsule when Leo has never even been here before," I said.

"That's not my story to tell," said Simone.

"Well, the editor isn't *mine*," I said.

Simone glanced at me. "Your sister . . . she's real sick, huh? Your mom said you guys were close."

I didn't respond. I was tired; I was so *tired* of people trying to grab on to pieces of Blair. Aleksander and Father Peter Patrick and Miss Mae and Harrison and Joe at the hardware store. Everyone wanted to hold on to her and make her their own story. Well, she was *my* sister. Not some freak show of the week.

"I'm sorry," she said. "I don't mean to bring her up. It's just—I have a sister, too. We're close. It must be hard."

I reached up and tightened my ponytail. "I see Leo."

We got to the clearing, where Leo stood with a telescope pointed toward the sky. Not the Star-Gazer Twelve, obviously, but his Tyler-Weimer, which was almost as good.

"Sagittarius," he said, pointing. "The archer. Easy to find for an astronomer like yourself, yes?"

It was. It was a whole pile of stars, right there in the sky. When I tried to point out constellations to my mom or Jade, they would just squint their eyes and shake their heads. But to me, they seemed clear as day.

"We wanted to go over the plan for Saturday," said

Leo. "I think it's smart if you double-check with the librarian. See what she knows."

"And then it won't be super obvious when the time capsule gets dug up?" I asked. "I thought that was the whole point of the metal detectors! I could have asked her right away!"

"Why would *you* dig it up? You're a kid, kids talk," said Leo, waving his hand dismissively, ignoring my logic. "No one will jump to conclusions about you. The item missing is of no importance to a little girl."

"Little girl? I'm going to be in eighth grade," I told him. "Besides, everyone knows I like the stars."

"Is there even a record of what's in it? Maybe no one will notice it's missing," said Simone. "At any rate, would they dig it up again if they thought it had been dug up? I mean, it's not like there's ten thousand dollars hidden in there."

"Actually, the telescope is worth—well. Never mind that. The eclipse will only be a few minutes long. Obviously it will take us a bit longer than that to fully retrieve it, so every single moment is precious. We don't have time for you to be running around willy-nilly with a shovel. We have to be sure," said Leo.

"We *are* sure. That spot was the only place the metal

detectors picked anything up," I said.

Leo threw his hands in the air. "And perhaps it's nothing! A faulty detector, a dropped quarter that got buried over the years, a *pipe*!" His eyes were blazing. This was serious business to him. Life or death.

"I think Simone should be there, too," Leo continued.

"What?" Simone and I asked in unison.

"This type of manual labor may require two people," he argued.

"No," I insisted, "I can *do* it."

"Besides, you need me to help coordinate your interviews," said Simone. "Last time you talked to a reporter without me, you went off on a tangent about whether or not Pluto was a planet."

"Well, that's actually a fascinating—"

"The interview was about a meteor shower, Leo!" she said, exasperated. "You need to focus. See what I mean?" Sometimes, I couldn't believe how Simone talked to Leo. It was like she was his mom instead of his employee. I wasn't sure who needed who more.

"I can handle getting the telescope," I assured him again. "I've got this."

Leo fidgeted, crossing his arms. "The eclipse will begin at 2:12 p.m. on the dot," he said. "We'll be at the viewing party. Your town board has actually asked me to deliver a brief talk beforehand. Someone caught wind I was an astronomer. CNN will be there, too; I'm doing an interview. It's the perfect alibi. While I'm speaking, you'll be digging. Thirty minutes should be plenty of time for you to complete the task, if you're that confident about your strength. We'll meet directly after the eclipse back at Eagle's Nest. You give me the telescope, I give you the previously determined payment of an introduction to Joanna. We part ways, both satisfied."

Except I was missing the greatest astronomical event of my lifetime, and my dad would be having a heart attack.

Blair, I reminded myself. This was for my sister. Mom and Jade thought they could save Blair by looking at old pictures and buying a fresh coat of paint. I was actually doing something about it. Maybe she wouldn't be a famous dancer, but we could show the world Captain Moonbeard. It wasn't ballet, but it would have to do.

Leo stepped away from the telescope and motioned for me to have a look.

Those stars, that light—so far away. Already dead. But I couldn't stop looking.

"It's weird," I said. "That they're already dead."

"What?" asked Leo, sounding confused.

"The stars," I said. "They're dead. We're seeing them how they used to be."

He shook his head. "No. Not always."

"What?"

He waved a hand. "One of those Twitter facts. Who told you stars were dead? Tell me it wasn't someone who actually calls themselves an *educator*."

"We don't do astronomy in school," I said.

He snorted. "Of course you don't. It's too important. Honestly, the American school systems . . ."

Simone rolled her eyes. Leo had a handful of rants, from the American School System to People Who Let Their Dogs Off Their Leash to Why Would Anyone Watch Football When Cricket Is So Much More Dignified.

"You *are* seeing light how it used to be," he said. "And stars do die. But their life spans are long—a million years or so, oftentimes. It only takes light a few years to get from here to there—and that's for stars that are far away. Most of the ones you're seeing right now are still in the sky, happily burning."

I looked back through the telescope, taking in the still-shining stars. When I pulled away, Leo was standing with his arms crossed, just staring up at the sky.

"After all these years, this is still my favorite way to look at them," he said. "With my own two eyes."

I tipped my head back. It was mine, too.

"They feel so close in the telescope. It's freaky," said Simone. "It's like if we yell loud enough, the aliens living on them can hear us."

"There couldn't be aliens on stars," I said. "They're burning balls of gas."

Leo smiled at me. "Don't mind her. She studies Shakespeare."

"You do? I thought you were, like, a teaching assistant," I said, surprised.

"Please. I'm his *personal* assistant; I schedule his speaking gigs and stuff. Answer his emails. All of this science talk? Nah. Shakespeare, now, that's worth your time," said Simone. "*By the pricking of my thumbs, something wicked this way comes.* The man had a way with words. Astronomy . . . it's math. It's dull."

"*Dull*," said Leo, chortling. I read that word in a book once—*chortling*—and wasn't sure what it meant. But when I heard the sound Leo made, there was no other word to describe it. That was a chortle. "Dull! As if the entirety of the universe was dull. As if *human existence* could possibly be dull. The study of our galaxy is the most passionate study there is."

I didn't know who to agree with. I liked the stars *because* they were dependable and set in stone. But now, maybe, they weren't.

"One day," Simone said to Leo, "I'm going to quit working for you, and you're not even going to be able to find your shoes—"

"That's true," he admitted. "I wouldn't last an afternoon."

"And I'm going to teach," she told me. "*Macbeth*, *King Lear* . . ."

"Maybe I'll take one of your classes," I said with a grin.

"No," said Leo, grabbing his heart jokingly. "Don't join the dark side!"

I laughed. "I'm sorry, was that a very lame attempt at a Star Wars quote?"

"*Aliens!*" yelled Simone, making me jump. "*Are you out there?*" She yelled across the lake, up to the sky. A dog barked.

"*We come in peace!*" yelled Leo. Simone and I cracked up. The proper professor, in his British accent, howling to the moon.

"*Welcome to Earth!*" I yelled as loud as I could.

"*Shut up!*" someone shouted from a window at Paul

Bunyan's. We laughed, harder than Mom and Jade with the pictures. Simone was doubled over as Leo responded loudly with a word I wasn't allowed to say, and she hissed "*Leo!*" through her laughter.

"It feels good! It feels good to *yell*," said Leo. "Mercy, sometimes you just want to . . . ," and he let loose, a roar, a ripping thunder of sound across the lake. Even with voice raised he had an accent. Simone yelled, too, and before I knew it, I did the same. We were making so much noise, taking up space in this gigantic universe where we were just little dots, specks of dust floating around in a ginormous galaxy. And Leo discovered new planets and the galaxy grew and when it did, we shrank smaller and smaller. Just like Blair, shrinking into nothing, going from the shiniest star I knew to a thinner and thinner and thinner dash of light.

I yelled and I yelled, as loud as I could get. I yelled all the way to the moon. I yelled all the way to the stars. And when Simone and Leo stopped and looked at me, I kept yelling.

"Abby," said Leo nervously, "maybe—"

"Stop," said Simone harshly, holding up a hand. "You let her yell." She turned back to me. "Go ahead, girl. You tell that sky what's what."

And so I did: I screamed, across the lake, across Wisconsin, all the way to Blair. Was this how she had felt on Memorial Day, yelling across Main Street, sending her voice to the sky? I yelled so loud I would scare Anna Rexia out of our house and out of our lives. Because after everything Blair had done, and after everything we'd been through, here I was: screaming for her to come back, and screaming for her to stay away.

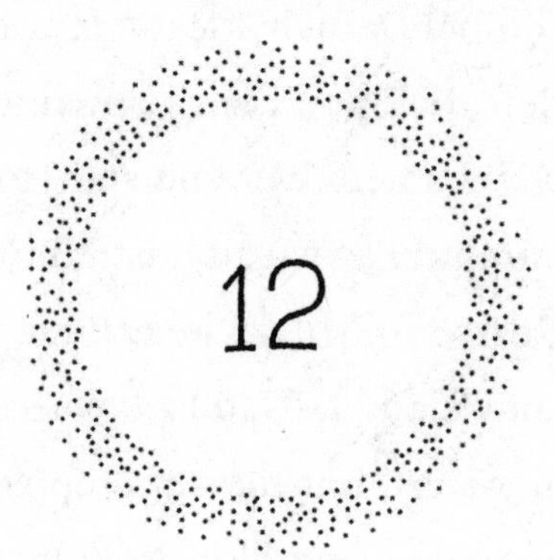

SEPTEMBER, THREE YEARS AGO

Nine years old

Three years before I screamed across Fishtrap Lake, setting fire to my vocal cords and waking up the fireflies, Dr. Leo Lacamoire was an accomplished astronomer preparing for a TED Talk. He was something, that Dr. Lacamoire: traveling the world for speeches, writing books about stars, always searching for new planets. Something terrible would happen to him soon, but he did not know that yet. All he knew was his fame and his fortune and his fans, each of them clamoring for a piece of the greatest scientist in the US.

It was September, which meant it was light out at 5:30 when we left to go see Blair's opening-night performance of *Coppélia*. There were no stars to be seen, and it still felt like summer as we all hustled into the car and made the long drive to Milwaukee. Blair was Swanilda, the girl whose boyfriend falls in love with a doll. I mean, seriously? Spoiler alert, but they end up getting married anyway. I say if a guy starts liking a doll more than you, you better hightail it to the hills. Call the cops, cause that guy's messed up. But I was only nine then. I wasn't thinking of things like that. I was thinking of Blair, in one of the lead roles, and of the many extra lessons she'd had with Aleksander to perfect it. I was thinking of the fact that Mom said we couldn't spend the whole weekend in Milwaukee at a hotel like we sometimes did because of all the money it had cost for Blair's private lessons and tutu and shoes. But it was all for Blair, who had recently slid the latest chapter of *Planet Pirates* under my bedroom door and who French-braided my and Sophie's hair for fun last weekend at our sleepover. I would drive a million miles there and back just to see her.

The theater was crowded. It was one of those ritzy places with plush seats and little boxes in the corner that you imagine kings and queens sitting in. When we sat down, I pulled out the program Mom had bought. There was Blair, smiling in a picture, with too much makeup on.

> *Last seen as an Arabian dancer in The Nutcracker, Blair McCourt trains at Aleksander Alekseev's Milwaukee School for Classical Ballet. She is a freshman at Waukegan County High School. Much love to Mom, Dad, Jade, and Abby.*

There our names were, right there in print! I knew instantly that I would keep it, forever. We'd look back at it in fifty years when Blair was a professional dancer.

We waited patiently for the show to start, and when it did—

Well.

She stole the show.

That's what everyone told us after. *Blair stole the show*, the other parents in the lobby said, giving Mom tight hugs. The write-up in the *Milwaukee Journal Sentinel* said the same thing, that although Kevin Krier danced beautifully as Franz and Dr. Coppélius was played by the exquisite Brandon Johansson, Blair McCourt as Swanilda was the one who stole the show.

I asked Mom what that meant, and she said it meant

that the audience's attention went to Blair because she was the best. Mom said this so proudly, even though I thought it might be a little mean. After all, everyone had worked so hard. Was Blair blocking the light from all those other people, even the dancers who were mainly just in the background?

But it was true. She did steal the show. What she did, the way she could move, was more than ballet. It was magic. I'd seen Blair dance a thousand times before, but this was different. She had switched from *pretty good* to *amazing.* To watch something like that happen—someone tell a story through turns and leaps and pirouettes—was like watching something transform. Blair wasn't just talented, I realized, sitting in that theater. She wasn't just *good*, the way I was good at spelling and Dad was good at fixing things. Blair was magnificent. Blair really did have a *destiny.*

And yet. There was something else, too. Ballet suddenly seemed so *beautiful.* I knew that other people saw it that way—that dance was for pretty girls in pretty costumes with pretty lights. Ballet had always been so ugly in my eyes: the way it tore Blair's feet to shreds, the way her shoulder blades stuck out when she stretched, the way sweat dripped from her forehead after practice.

Blair, grimacing while Aleksander yanked her feet into a firmer arch—*that* was how I had thought ballet could make you feel. It was as glamorous as wrestling to me. But when Blair was on that stage, playing Swanilda, you couldn't deny it: she was beautiful.

The day before, I saw her standing in front of the mirror in her room, just looking at herself. Her face was less than an inch away from the glass, and her hands were pushed against it. She was staring so intensely, like she could burn a hole through the glass if she tried. Then she made a face—one of disgust. It was as if she had stepped in Obi's poop. Her lip curled up, eyes glaring, totally horrified. Yes, she was beautiful, but no, she couldn't see it. That much I knew. I had never seen Blair make that face before, but it was far from the last time.

On the way home from her opening-night performance, we stopped for ice cream. Blair got two scoops of Moose Tracks, our favorite, which I still remember because I spilled some of mine in the back seat and she shared the rest of hers. Jade was in a good mood, too, even though she had just started seventh grade and kind of seemed to hate everybody and everything. She ordered Blue Moon, a flavor I wished I liked because of the cool name, but it actually tasted like stale Lucky Charms.

"Magnificent," Mom said, kissing her fingers and mimicking Aleksander. "This girl is a star!"

"Better than I've seen, even in all my days in Russia," Dad drawled. "A measly American!"

"Stop," Blair howled. "I'm gonna pee my pants."

"That man, Blair! He's something else. How you spend so much time with him, I will never know. But he's definitely taught you well. You were *superb*," Mom said.

"The best dancer by far," Dad added.

"I was not," said Blair, blushing. She was. We all knew it, including her.

"That guy you had to dance with looked like he needed to take the stick out of his butt, though," said Jade.

Dad and Blair cracked up, but Mom reached back and flicked Jade on the knee. "Jade Marie! Watch the language!"

"I just said *butt*!" We were all sugar-drunk and exploded in laughter again.

"Ooh, listen to what's on! Our jam!" Mom cranked the radio.

"Mom. Do not say jam. It's not 1985," said Jade. But she started wiggling with anticipation. It *was* our jam.

"Not Dolly Parton," groaned Dad, covering his ears.

Mom *loved* Dolly Parton. This was her favorite song, about Dolly's mom taking a bunch of rags and making her a coat in a bunch of different colors. I always found her humming it while she washed dishes or dusted the bookshelves, shaking her hips in a way that made Jade beg her to stop.

"Back through the years I go wanderin' once again . . . ," sang Mom.

"*Back to the seasons of my youth!*" Blair and I shrieked. Jade rolled her eyes, but she was grinning.

"I recall a box of rags that someone gaaaaave us," sang Mom, snapping her fingers.

"*And how my mama put those rags to use!*"

I had seen a documentary about Dolly Parton once. Mom made me watch it with her, but I actually kind of liked it. She was from Locust Ridge, a town not much smaller than Moose Junction. Even when she was little, everyone knew she was special. They were just waiting for the day she'd make it big.

She was a blond-haired, long-nailed, southern-drawled version of my sister, really. Blair was too good for Moose Junction, Wisconsin. She would take off one day, leaving us all behind, and charge into some unknown future where people would throw flowers at her feet and beg for her autograph. Something about that made me feel queasy. Mom and Dad were just so proud to be Blair's parents, beaming as everyone praised her and framing the reviews from *Coppélia*. Jade acted like she didn't care at all. But I felt nervous. If Blair left, which she obviously would one day, who would we be, if not her family? Who was I, Abigail Leigh McCourt, if not Blair's little sister?

Just as I thought that, Blair threw her arm around me and gave me a loud, ice-cream-filled kiss on the cheek. I shrieked and ripped away. Who was I if not Blair's little sister? Maybe I would never have to find out.

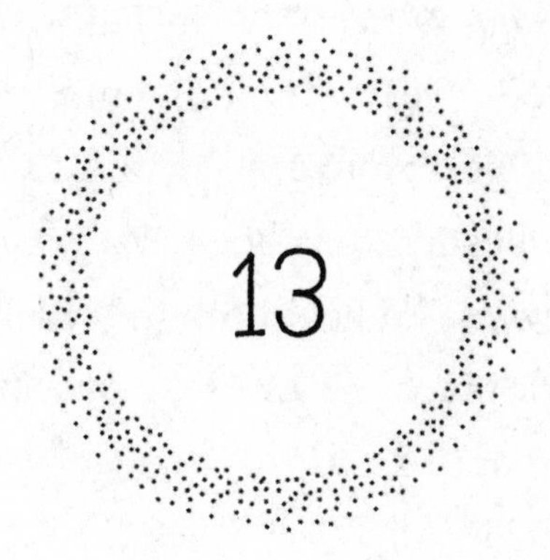

AUGUST, PRESENT DAY

Twelve years old

The next morning, I swung by the library to see if Harriet had gotten the new *Starkeeper* book yet. I had barely passed the reference desk when I saw him—Caleb Evers, dropping a couple of books into the return slot.

I froze, but he looked up and saw me. We just kind of stared at each other for a second, until he awkwardly raised a hand.

"Hey," he said.

My grand plan of evaporating into thin air didn't seem to be working.

"Hey," I said. I pointed at the book he was returning,

A Gardener's Guide to Herbs. "New hobby?"

He chuckled. "Just running some errands for my mom. Sucking up before I head to La Crosse." That's where he was headed to college. *One thousand, one hundred and four miles*, I'd heard him tell Blair once as they sat on our back porch. *La Crosse to New York. Not so far.* She hadn't responded.

"Soon, right?"

"Soon," he said. "A couple of weeks. I'm going to miss this place."

"I'd think you couldn't wait to leave," I said. Then I felt stupid. Sure, Blair was gone, but his parents were here. His friends. His life. It's not like he was all alone.

He gave a half smile. "I should head out."

"See ya," I said, turning around.

"Um. Abby? Actually . . ."

I stopped.

He looked at his shoes. "How's Blair doing?"

I felt like we'd been through something, me and Caleb. We'd both loved someone fiercely and let them slip through our fingers.

But I wished she understood, in her room at Harvest Hills, that this thing? It wasn't just about her. She may have been the star ballerina, but we were all her backup dancers, perfecting our turns and memorizing our choreography. Anna Rexia had dug her claws into all of us.

"I don't know," I said honestly. "I haven't gone to see her."

"You haven't?" He was surprised. "But . . . you guys are so close."

That photo flashed in my mind: me, Blair, and Jade on Halloween. The Sanderson sisters. Are close. Were close.

"Sorry," he said. "That would probably be really hard. To go see her someplace she doesn't belong."

I nodded. He understood.

"Maybe you could write her a letter or something," he said.

"Maybe. Mom said she's doing pretty good. She'll be home really soon, actually."

"That's . . . that's good. I—" He inhaled. "Just tell her I said hi. Whenever you see her. Okay?"

"You could visit her, I bet," I said lamely. "If you called first."

He smiled that Caleb Evers smile, the one that should be in movies. But it didn't meet his eyes.

"No," he said. "I don't think that's a good idea. But you tell her hi for me."

"I will," I said.

"I'll see you around, Abby."

I wanted to ask him if he remembered the popcorn from the movies and the fun we'd had. But he turned and walked away.

I was about to kneel down and grab the first *Starkeeper* off the shelf, thinking a little reread could tide me over if Harriet hadn't ordered the new release yet, when a big blue eye peered at me from the other side of the shelf.

"Leo!" I said. "You practically gave me a heart attack."

"Abigail! What a surprise," he said loudly before lowering his voice to a whisper. "How was the mission? Successful?"

"No. I mean, yes, I'll ask, but—*no*, I just like the library! That's why I'm here! God. You have got to chill," I said, shaking my head.

Leo cleared his throat and beckoned toward Harriet, who was shelving some picture books.

His expression commanded: *Go.*

Crap. Now I was stuck.

I walked over to her quickly, anxious to get this over with.

"Hey," I said.

"Hi, Abby. How's it going?"

I looked her straight in the face and asked if there was a time capsule buried outside, showing her the article Leo had found. Clearly confused, she nodded slowly.

"You're not thinking of doing anything foolish, are you, Abby?" she said. "Something you shouldn't?"

"No," I said. "It's for a summer school project. The history of Moose Junction." But she didn't believe me, I could tell. And she shouldn't have. But I would get ahold of Joanna Creech, even if I got in trouble first.

"Okay. Well. You let me know if you need help," she said. "Didn't know you had summer school this year."

"It's online," I lied. Apparently, some mystery class that involved metal detectors and history projects. "By the way, do you have the new *Starkeeper* book yet? It came out last weekend."

"I'm sorry, Abby, but I can't order any more books this year. You may have to wait until your birthday."

Great. Not only did I have to lie to the face of one of the only friends I had left, but I wouldn't even get a new book to escape into?

I hurried back to Leo, giving him a look that clearly said, *Happy?*

"Relax. I wasn't here to check up on you. By the way, the nonfiction section of this library is abysmal. I'm doing research for my latest book, and I can't find anything that isn't about different types of tree bark."

I glared at him. You don't insult the Moose Junction Library in front of me. "Harriet can only buy a few books a year. She has to be very selective. Besides, if you're looking for books on space, why are you over here in fiction?"

He smiled. "Well. I've been busted. I'm really here to find the latest Elaine Luther mystery. But I'm all turned around."

"You read mysteries?" Something about that surprised me.

"Do I detect a hint of *judgment*? Mysteries are an art form, Abigail. Not like this space-magic garbage you young kids always want to read."

Okay, *that* made me mad. "For your information, science fiction isn't garbage. It's the combination of imagination and the growing world around us." Okay, I had stolen that from Harriet after hearing her snap at someone who had once insulted the genre.

He snorted. "Really? All I see are lovestruck teenagers on spaceships."

"Then you aren't looking hard enough." I knelt down and found the first *Starkeeper* book. "Here," I said after getting back up and handing it to him. "Everyone knows you can't just browse shelves at eye level. The best books hide on the bottom."

"Is that so," he said flatly. But he was smiling.

"Yes. If you're going to read sci-fi, do it right."

He took the book and held it for a minute, just looking at it.

"I knew someone once who loved these books," he said kind of sadly. "I've never read them."

"That's what libraries are for," I told him. "It's not too late."

"No," he said absentmindedly, "I suppose it never is."

School was starting in only a couple of weeks, which meant plenty of things: fewer tourists, a long, lonely bus ride, and boots instead of flip-flops. But it also meant a trip to Target . . . usually. Mom and Dad hadn't spent a lot of money this summer. Even though the eclipse was going to bring in "the big bucks," as Joe from Hank's Hardware said, I think Blair's hospital place was costing even more. It had something to do with insurance. The phone rang with a Madison number about once a week, and Mom would roll her eyes and groan *insurance* before talking angrily to someone for an hour. Plus we were getting bills in the mail, but like half of them were wrong and Mom would have to call the Madison guy *again*.

So basically, Blair, after costing a billion dollars to do ballet, was now costing a billion dollars to *not* do ballet. And that meant fewer trips to the Ice Shanty, no movies unless Jade could give us coupons, and the Cheerios that aren't really Cheerios.

So when Mom asked if I wanted to do our Target trip the next day, I was pretty excited. The nearest Target was close to two hours away, in Washport. We could have gone to the Walmart in Waukegan or ordered stuff online, but we only went to Target—or *Tarjay*, as my mom called it—once a year. Even Jade came. It was a big deal; we could get pretzel bites and Icees from the café and buy basically any school supplies we wanted, plus some new clothes. My jeans from last year were too short, and I was already pretty high on the Dork-O-Meter: I didn't need high-water jeans to seal my fate. I could see on Instagram that everyone was wearing cool sneakers instead of flats, which everyone had worn last year. I liked back-to-school shopping, which made me think that I belonged on the Dork-O-Meter after all. But that fresh-notebook smell: I was helpless. Give me some new #2 pencils and I was in heaven.

I was surprised when Jade didn't even complain about going, since almost every second of her summer that she wasn't working had been spent with her friends. Jade wouldn't invite me within thirty feet of her coven (Mr. Linn taught us that a *coven* meant a group of witches, something I found pretty accurate), but since it was thunderstorming out, I guess she didn't mind spending most of her day in a car with Mom and me. Dad stayed behind to check some new eclipse viewers into their cabins.

When you go to Target all the time, you can probably just pop in, grab what you want, and pop out. But we had a *routine.* A Target plan, if you will. Always start in cosmetics, make your way to movies and music, check out the seasonal area, where the school supplies currently were, and then head over into the clothing department before swinging down the home decor aisle. It was an art form.

"We need to see if they have this new series I'm reading," I said. "Harriet said the library couldn't order the new one because she was already over her book limit. I'll spend my own money on it."

Mom sighed. "That library. You need to prepare yourself, Abigail. I'm not sure how much longer it's going to be around."

"Why?" asked Jade, picking up a glittery black nail polish that Mom grabbed out of her hands and put back on the shelf.

Nail polish brought a million flashes of Blair to my mind. She'd use clear nail polish to fix runs in her tights. It was also the only color Aleksander allowed on her fingers. She went through a bottle a week.

"Jade Marie, I love you, but black nails?" Mom asked, pulling me out of my memory and back down to earth. "Don't turn into one of those emo kids on me. I have enough to deal with." Turning back to me, she continued, "The town's funding has been hit hard. The library isn't a big tourist attraction."

I shook my head so hard my ponytail whipped my cheeks. "They can't close the library!"

"Well, it's obviously not up to me, sweet pea. Your dad has a town selectman council meeting tonight where they're making the final decision. I just wanted to warn you."

I groaned. Mom got my love of the library about as much as she got my love of space.

"You should spend more time hanging out with actual kids instead of a librarian, anyway," said Jade, picking up another shade of dark polish. "What about navy?"

"Fine. One. You want a color, Abigail?"

But I couldn't pay attention to things like nail polish when the only place I really felt at home these days was in danger of closing. And what about Harriet? Where would she go? What if I never saw her again and the last thing I ever did was lie to her?

I could feel a lump rising in my throat, and let's just say I did *not* want to be the weirdo crying at Target. But seriously? First Blair, and now this?

"Oh, Abigail. I'm sorry. I shouldn't have told you that right now. I didn't mean to ruin our trip." Mom bit her lip. "I'll buy you that book, okay?"

"It's not—" I shook my head. How could I explain it wasn't one book? It was all the books. It was past and current and future books, books that gave me hours away from my current, stupid life. Books that were there when nothing else was.

"Isn't that Sophie and Lex?" asked Jade. My head snapped up.

What were the odds? I mean, really. We were close to two hours away from home. Not exactly light-years, but still. Yet there they were, looking at the hair products, giggling at something.

"What a surprise! Go say hi," said Mom.

Crap. I either had to stand there and awkwardly explain to my mom and sister that I didn't really have any friends for a reason I still hadn't figured out, or go over to my two "best friends" who hadn't so much as texted me all summer and were apparently having a Target bestie day. Like, would you rather have Kylo Ren or Voldemort standing in front of you?

I walked over to them cautiously, trying to keep my voice down so Mom and Jade couldn't hear.

"Um. Hey."

They saw me and froze. Lex even dropped the bottle she was holding and had to quickly bend down and get it, and when she did *that*, she knocked a whole bunch of shampoos off the shelf.

"Hi, Abby," said Sophie, biting her lip. "What are you doing here?"

"I'm with Mom and Jade," I said.

"The Tarjay extravaganza," said Sophie, smiling, not in a mean way. Of course she knew we did this every year. She'd even come with us before.

"What have you guys been up to?" I asked nervously.

They looked at each other and then back at me. I willed for a lightning bolt to strike.

"Not much," said Sophie simply.

"Come on," said Lex, tugging on her elbow. "We should go. My mom's waiting for us at Starbucks."

"Bye, Abby," said Sophie.

"Bye," chirped Lex. They hurried away as if I had some kind of disease they were afraid of catching. I resisted the urge to check my teeth or sniff my armpits. I mean, seriously?

The rest of the trip I was in a bad mood, the kind of mood that hangs over you like a cloud and makes everyone around you grumpy, too. Jade and Mom fought over what kind of pens she needed for school, if she could buy a tank top that was kind of see-through, and whether or not a sixteen-year-old should be drinking coffee. I just picked out the bare minimum amount of notebooks and threw the first pair of jeans I saw into the cart without even trying them on. I felt bad for my mom. One daughter didn't eat, one daughter argued over everything, and one daughter was a loser freak liar with no friends. She'd played the genetics lottery and lost.

As we drove home, Mom turned on the radio. "Coat of Many Colors" came on, but we didn't sing along. Not a single word.

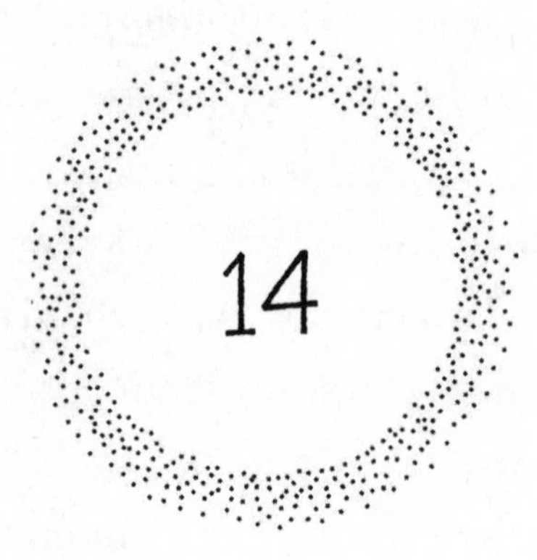

JUNE, THREE YEARS AGO

Nine years old

Three years and two months before that ill-fated Tarjay trip, Dr. Leo Lacamoire was beginning his summer class at MIT, an in-depth study of gamma-ray bursts. He was deciding on the title of his next book and whether he should have red or white wine at lunch. Those were the concerns of Dr. Leo Lacamoire, PhD, back then.

Blair had just begun *Coppélia* rehearsals. It was one of her first leading roles. Jade had discovered the art of texting on her shiny new cell phone, falling off the face of the earth. Sophie and Lex were my best friends, and we had just finished fourth grade.

I was lying on the dock with Blair, something that was becoming more and more uncommon. Even then, she was stretching, pulling her toes over her head in a way that didn't seem human. I was nine years old and wanted to go swimming, not lie there. But my sister had just sprayed something in her hair to give it beach waves or whatever and said she couldn't go in the water, so I had a book, like always. I'm sorry, but what's with girls not wanting to get their hair wet? That's the dumbest thing I've ever heard. It was eighty billion degrees, too hot to sprawl out on a towel.

Where was Jade? Who knew. She was thirteen, a teenager, now, with a gaggle of friends and no time for her sisters. She'd said she might come later, but she probably wouldn't. She had become tight with some girls from school, and they were clearly a lot more fun than her own family.

"How's your book?" asked Blair, waving as a boat of fishermen puttered by.

I shook my head. "Blah, blah, magic, blah, blah, love, blah blah, time travel. Boring."

She laughed and pulled out her sketchbook.

"What are you working on?" I asked her. Blair was amazing at drawing. Better than she was at dance, even, but then—I hadn't seen her in *Coppélia* yet.

"Fan art," she said, showing me a picture of Padmé Amidala with a smirk on her face. "Don't you ever just wish Anakin had stayed good, and they could have had their twins and lived happily ever after?"

"Um, no. Then we wouldn't have Star Wars." I flipped through her sketchbook. Pictures of Padmé, Katniss, Black Widow, Hermione and Ron, Aria from *Pretty Little Liars*, which Mom said I couldn't watch but I sometimes did with Blair anyway. Some of real people—Misty Copeland, her idol. Mom, laughing. Aleksander, a scowl on his face. And then, over and over again, a character I didn't recognize.

"Who is this?" I asked, pointing to her. She was a tall, thin girl, maybe Blair's age, with a full, shimmery skirt and long curls.

"Oh," said Blair, looking kind of embarrassed. "I made her up. It's stupid."

I kept flipping. "This is awesome," I said, running my hands over the pictures. "What's her name?"

"I don't know," she said. "I can see her, but that's all."

She was in a spaceship, doing a pirouette on the moon, kissing a guy who looked kind of like Draco Malfoy.

Blair reached over and grabbed a handful of chips. They were sour cream and onion, our favorite. Was she already counting calories then, pinching her sides in her swimsuit? Had Anna Rexia been hiding under the dock and whispering up between the boards about trans fats? I don't know.

"I love her," I said. "She needs a name."

"I think she's a princess," said Blair.

I nodded, stealing her pencil. I added some captions.

Princess Stardust flies to her home planet, Andor.

Princess Stardust and Antoine Moonbeard.

Princess Stardust dancing on the moon.

"Princess Stardust," laughed Blair. "I like it."

We made up an adventure for her, filling pages with sketches and words. She could go anywhere we wanted. We didn't have to wait for Marvel or J. K. Rowling or the comic books to tell us what happened next. We dripped chip dust and Mountain Dew onto her sketchbook pages, but Blair didn't care. She drew quickly and loved the stories I made up. We spent hours on the dock that day, getting so sunburned my mom had to go buy a real aloe plant for our backs.

From then on, *Planet Pirates* was our thing. Blair

always started it, sketching out some comic squares of Princess Stardust, and I trailed closely behind, filling in the story. Jade might have floated away. But as always, Blair led, and I followed. She was my sister—I would have followed her anywhere.

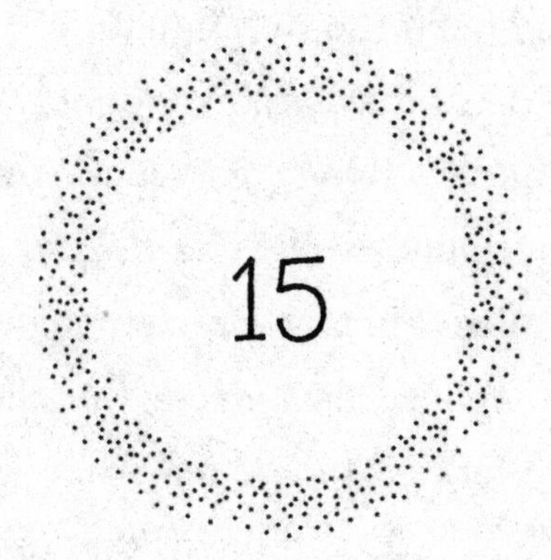

AUGUST, PRESENT DAY

Twelve years old

It was the day before the eclipse, and you would have thought the president was coming to Moose Junction.

The entire town was buzzing, and I mean *buzzing*. News cameras had arrived on Main Street, with Miss Mae talking to whoever had a camera about the communists. Mom and Dad barely had time to sit, they were so busy fixing leaks and delivering extra pillowcases and handing out tourist information. Jade spent all her time either at the movie theater or running around with her friends. Harriet started a petition to keep the library open and sat out front every day, talking to anyone who walked by. I had been the first signature.

"Signatures don't make money appear, Abby," Dad had told me tiredly. "Don't get your hopes up." The meeting had not gone well. The decision was pushed until October, after there'd been enough time to see what boost the eclipse had given. But the library was not deemed a priority. We needed a new game warden, some potholes covered, a stoplight that didn't questionably flicker during thunderstorms. Dusty books were something that could be crossed off the list. Dad had told me this the night before, putting a massive bowl of ice cream in front of me and breaking the bad news.

"You could have fought for it," I said through tears.

"Oh, Abs," he said with a sigh. "I tried. But I'm just one person."

"You're a very respected member of the community," I said. "That's what your little biography thing on the town website says."

"I'm a very respected member of the community who understands the importance of traffic lights *and* a robust fiction section," he said.

But there was Harriet, full of hope. Dreams weren't dashed just yet. The October deadline seemed ages away.

Well, I'd learned my lesson in the hope department. It

was the rest of my family who had theirs up. Every second Mom wasn't walking someone wearing a Chicago Bears sweatshirt to their cabin, she was redecorating Blair's room. She had painted it light blue and hung up a poster of Rey from Star Wars where Misty Copeland had been. Blair's old tutus, ones that had cost hundreds of dollars and been painstakingly sewed and detailed, were in a box in the garage next to the Christmas decorations. It was like Mom thought if she took a sponge to ballet and scrubbed it out of our lives, Blair would magically go back to normal.

Final plans for the telescope had been made. During the eclipse—the moment I'd been waiting ages for, that I probably wouldn't see again for years—I would be at the library, supposedly digging up the time capsule and retrieving the telescope. Dr. Lacamoire would be giving an interview for CNN, a perfect alibi.

"God, it's hot here," said Simone, tying her long hair into a ponytail. "Isn't Wisconsin supposed to be cold?" We were standing on the back porch of Eagle's Nest.

"Um. It's August," I pointed out as gently as possible. "We're in the Northwoods, not Antarctica."

She sighed. "I'm supposed to get some iced coffee with your mom in a few minutes. I'm forcing her to take a break. Between getting things ready for your sister and making sure all of your cabins are good to go, she's about to pass out. I've never met a woman who works so hard."

I nodded. It was true. She was like the Energizer Bunny these days.

"You didn't tell me your sister was a dancer," Simone said.

I shrugged.

"When your mom first said so, I thought she meant, like, cheerleader. Dance team or whatever. But she was a *real* dancer, huh? Ballet—that's tough stuff. Not for the weak."

Tough? Blair cried over carbs. She used to be tough, sure, but now she was about as tough as a butterfly. I just shrugged again. Simone took the hint.

"So, you're all set. You have the shovel. Tomorrow, during the eclipse, you're on time capsule duty," said Simone.

Leo, who was usually so involved in the plan, was staring off into space. He seemed a million miles away.

"Leo? You've promised CNN an exclusive," said Simone. "Are you alive over there? Did you two take a vow of silence of something?"

Leo snapped back to attention. "Yes. It gets hot in August."

Simone and I groaned.

Leo shook his head. "I'm sorry. I am! I just . . . it's so close. The Star-Gazer Twelve, it's . . ." He held out his hand. "It's right there. But so much could go wrong. You could get busted," he said, nodding at me. "Or—or maybe it's not even there."

"It will be there," said Simone confidently.

My stomach dropped. "But if it's not . . . ," I said.

"Why would you say that? Of course it will be there," said Simone, shaking her head. "People! Come on! You're losing energy. The fight's almost over. We've almost got the thing back that you've been talking about for a year. Don't lose hope."

"Hope," scoffed Leo. "I'm a scientist. I deal in facts, not feelings."

I loved Leo even more then. I would get that telescope for him. I would! He had brought the adventure I'd been wishing for, and a book editor, too. What good was a telescope buried underground? It deserved to be looked through. It was probably lonely, buried down there with no one to appreciate it.

Simone sighed, shaking her head. "I've gotta meet Julie."

"I'm going to lie down," said Leo. "All of this excitement . . . it's hard on an old man." Leo was always referring to himself as an *old man*, even though he couldn't have been much older than my dad.

"Tomorrow," I said. "We meet here after the eclipse?"

"With the Star-Gazer Twelve," said Simone. "It's there, Leo. I promise."

I will, Mom. I promise.

But if Blair driving off to prom had taught me anything, it was that people don't always keep their promises, no matter how badly they want to.

Leo went inside and Simone took off. I walked down the steps of the patio and around the side of Eagle's Nest, smack into—

Jade.

A wide-eyed, can't-believe-it-looking Jade. A *spy* named Jade McCourt, clutching batteries.

"Jade!" I said. My face got hot and my heart started pounding.

"You're wearing my shirt," she said flatly.

For a second, I thought I'd gotten off easy. Her shirt was just an old Waukegan County High T-shirt. It had a *hole* in it, for cripes' sake. It wasn't like it was made of gold. If she wanted to be mad about me stealing a T-shirt, that was fine, as long as she hadn't heard us talking about—

"And you're digging up the time capsule," she said.

I stared at her.

"It's a long story . . . ," I said.

"To get the Star-Gazer Twelve," she said.

". . . one that apparently you already know," I finished meekly.

"Abby. Geez." She shook her head.

I pushed past her and ran home, hearing Jade run after me. I flung open our front door and sprinted up the stairs, wishing I had my own room, but of course, I didn't. Jade followed me in and sat next to me on my bed, just staring, out of breath, waiting for an explanation I didn't even have. I opened my mouth and shut it again. *He's giving me a chance. I can get* Planet Pirates *published, for real. I can give Blair something to be happy about. I can save her.*

Unfortunately, none of those things were true, and I knew it.

Blair and I weren't going to become famous comic book authors. You went to the store and you saw rows and rows of comics, most of them way better than ours. Blair was not going to go to New York City, either, to dance at the Joffrey. Blair was going to move home, where she'd measure her food and yell at my mom and cry in her bedroom. Dr. Leo Lacamoire would take the Star-Gazer Twelve and never speak to me again. It was going to be like last year, but worse. That's what was really going to happen.

When Mom was trying to get Blair to eat, she baked a lot. She made all of Blair's favorite things—apple pie with a homemade crust, blueberry muffins, lemon bars so tangy they made you wince. The best were these small powdered doughnuts in perfect balls she'd fry on the stove, filled with chocolate cream. They took forever to make and Blair wouldn't taste them; she wouldn't even take a single bite. I ate so many my stomach hurt.

But when you have a sister, that's what your life is like. On the inside of that sweet powdered doughnut, there is something hiding. Just like in the center of Blair's story—her story of sickness and *Coppélia* and *destiny*—was another story. The story of me, and Jade, and Mom and Dad, and even Obi. Hiding, tucked within the story that everyone else saw, was the story about how we were supposed to go on living when someone in our family was dying. Everyone saw Blair struggling but nobody thought for five seconds about what it was like to be sitting at that dinner table with her.

How was I supposed to be Abby McCourt, really? With no friends, no Blair, and a terrible, terrible lie in the pit of my stomach? Harriet was going to be furious. She'd know it was me, and I had lied to her: she would never speak to me again. Not that it would matter, because the library, the only place I ever loved in this stupid town, in this stupid state, on this stupid planet, was probably closing.

"Abby," said Jade. But it wasn't the exasperated *Abby* of stolen sweatshirts and snoring and forgetting to take Obi out. Or the *Abby* of *Grow up, Abby* and *Stop whining, Abby* and *Turn off the lights, Abby, I'm sleeping.*

It was an *I'm sorry, Abby.*

An *I understand, Abby.*

"I thought it would help Blair," I told her. I realized I had started crying. "I thought I could fix it."

She shook her head and put her hands on my shoulders. "Abby. You can't fix Blair. I can't fix Blair. Mom or Aleksander or the doctor or definitely Leo what's-his-face can't fix Blair. Only Blair can fix Blair."

"I thought of it like a person," I said, knowing I wasn't

really making sense. "Anna Rexia. Some freak witch that lives in our house."

"Really? Me, too, kind of," she said. "I thought of it like an energy. I saw this thing on TV once where people cleansed their house with smelling salts, and I told Mom we should do that before Blair came home."

"I have a plan," I told her fiercely, but she just shook her head.

"You're going to get busted. This is way too risky. Tell him to forget about it. Buy a new telescope, fancy doctor man. Move on."

"It's *his* telescope," I told her. "That's why he's here. He wants me to dig it up during the eclipse. He's been searching for it for years."

"Do you even have any proof it's his, Abby? Isn't it worth a million dollars? You're just going to *give* it to him, and say what? And say what to *Harriet*, who's going to know it was you when there's a big fresh dirt pile outside the library?"

"Leo and Simone will be halfway back to Massachusetts by then. And she won't know I helped them."

"She will," said Jade, "and you know it."

"Well, I haven't gotten that far," I bit out.

She sighed, pushing her hair behind her ears. She

had a new blue streak, bright, like the sky.

"This sucks," she said. "This whole summer. Without Blair. It sucks, doesn't it?"

I was surprised. "You don't even *like* Blair."

She cracked a smile. "Yeah, well, I don't like you, either. But that doesn't mean I don't love you, idiot."

She reached over to flick me on the temple and I batted her hand away.

"You two . . . you were always buddies. The same. I always felt like the third wheel," she said. "Mom told me I should just try to make some of my own friends. So I did."

I was surprised. "You never told me that."

She shrugged. "I don't like that nerd stuff. And Blair was always so defensive of you. I don't know, it made me mad sometimes. But—I don't have to be a jerk. I know that."

"I didn't think you missed her," I said.

"Hello? *I'm* the one who's been going to see her. I'm the one who's been talking about feelings with some lady who smells like cats in a therapist's office while Blair cries."

"Ew," I said.

"Tell me about it. Besides, maybe I don't miss Blair 2.0, who was always sad and wouldn't eat. But the first

Blair . . ." Jade grinned. "She was so fun. Wasn't she?"

"The most fun," I agreed. I felt tears poking my eyes. *Don't cry don't cry don't cry don't cry—*

"That time we were the Sanderson sisters for Halloween? Or the year we couldn't find sleds so we used Mom's baking trays, even though our butts could barely fit on them?" She shook her head. "Being her sister was like being . . ."

"On an adventure," I finished.

"Exactly. I thought for a while that we could get that first Blair back," said Jade. "If we—I don't know. Just pushed through. Like running a marathon or something. If we could just get rid of that stupid scale . . ."

The scale, shattered at the bottom of the garbage can.

"*You*," I said. "You threw that scale out!"

Jade squeezed her eyes shut. "Every morning, that thing would decide her mood for the day. Which Blair we were gonna get. I saw her on it in the bathroom one night at one a.m. when I had to pee. Who checks their weight at one a.m.?"

"I can't believe you did that," I said. "She'd kill you."

"It was dumb, though. One thing can't fix everything. And besides, we're *never* going to get the old Blair back." She flopped down on her bed and closed her eyes.

"We're going to get Blair 3.0 now. The one who's been through all of this craziness. Who knows what she'll be like?"

"What do you mean? Of course we can get her back. That's why she went away."

"No, it's not. She went away so we can go forward, not backward."

Blair, crying over cupcakes, and Jade, feeling left out, and me, lying and deceiving and sneaking around. We'd all been so different this summer. We were all more than the sliver of moon you can see from Earth.

"So don't do anything stupid, Abby," Jade said. "Or if you do . . . at least tell me first."

Later that day, I rode my bike to the library. I wanted to check in and see how Harriet's petition was coming, and besides, I was trying to avoid Mom and Dad. Every time one of them spotted me, I had to bring a guest bottled water or clean towels.

But as I coasted up to the library, I couldn't believe what I saw. It was Sophie, signing the petition at an empty table.

"Hey," I said, surprised. Sophie had never been a big library person.

She looked up, equally as stunned. "Abby. Hey." She waved the pen at me. "I'd ask you to sign, but you were probably first in line. It, um . . . it would suck. If the library had to close down. I know you like it here a lot," she said. She was holding her own helmet in one hand, and I saw her bike locked to a lamppost a few feet away.

"Did you come here just to do that?" I asked.

"I was going to grab some Sour Patch Kids at Coon-tail's," she said. "But the line was out the door. All of these people are here for the eclipse tomorrow."

"Yeah," I said awkwardly. We stood there for a minute in total silence. I kept waiting for her to hop on her bike and go, but she didn't.

"Well," I finally said, "you probably have plans for the day. With Lex or something."

She nodded. "We were going to go out in her boat with her parents."

"Oh."

"Her mom's been teaching me some Japanese this summer. It's been kind of fun."

"Cool." *Thanks for the invite.*

I turned to leave, but she stopped me.

"Abby. I—this is stupid. This whole summer of not

talking was stupid," she said quickly. "I'm sorry. Lex's mom and my mom said that you needed a break maybe, because of your sister being sick. That we should give you some space. Lex thought so, too. I think she got freaked out at Memorial Day. But I wasn't scared. I know Blair is just going through it. They talked to us about it in health class, remember?"

"Yeah." Our gym teacher, Mr. Fergus, taught health. He droned on about eating disorders for like ten minutes one day before reminding us of the dangers of obesity and heart disease. It wasn't exactly emphasized.

"I'm sorry. I should have called you. I don't want you to think we're not friends anymore." She bit her lip. "I mean, school starts in two weeks. And it's just us on the bus for so long. We're still friends, right?"

I could have said no. What kind of friend just ditches you for the whole summer? What kind of friend ignores you when you need her most?

But.

What kind of sister just ditches you for the whole summer? What kind of *sister* was I, ignoring Blair when she needed me? I wasn't being mean. I was scared. I was afraid things couldn't go back to the way they were. Sophie probably felt the same way.

"Yeah," I said. "Of course we're still friends. But thanks for saying sorry."

She looked relieved. "Want to come over on Sunday? If it's nice out we can do the paddleboards or something. All of the tourists will be on their way home."

I loved Sophie's house. Her mom always made the best snacks, and she had a big dog named Rufus that loved jumping in the lake. I grinned.

"I'll call you Sunday," I said.

As Sophie got on her bike and left, I felt that feeling wash over me again. *Hope:* that I still had friends. That I could get out of this time capsule mess. That Blair really could get better.

Stop it, a piece of me said. But another piece, a louder one, said, *Keep going. Keep going. Keep going.*

That night, as Jade drove off to the movie theater and Mom and Dad ran around making sure all the tourists were ready for tomorrow, I sat in bed and tried to write Blair a letter. I could write Captain Moonbeard into a thousand quests, but this seemed impossible.

What I really wanted to tell Blair was not that I was angry, even though part of me was. Or that I still loved her, even though I did. Or that I understood, even though I was trying to.

I wanted to tell her I was sorry.

I'm sorry you fell and none of us caught you.

I'm sorry I didn't tell Dad how scared I was the night you went to prom.

I'm sorry I believed you when you lied.

I'm sorry I thought you were too perfect to be struggling.

I'm sorry that I acted like you were a superstar instead of my sister.

I'm sorry.

I'm sorry.

I'm sorry.

I wrote them all out, apology after apology, my hand flying across the lines, my pencil practically digging into my notebook. I filled a page with regret and remorse. Then I tore it out, walked to the window, and ripped the letter into tinier and tinier pieces, letting them flutter to the ground. *Sorry for littering.* Add that one to the list. I would send my apologies to the trees and the birds and the lake and the woods itself, and maybe they'd burrow underground and find their way to my sister, sad and sick and stuck.

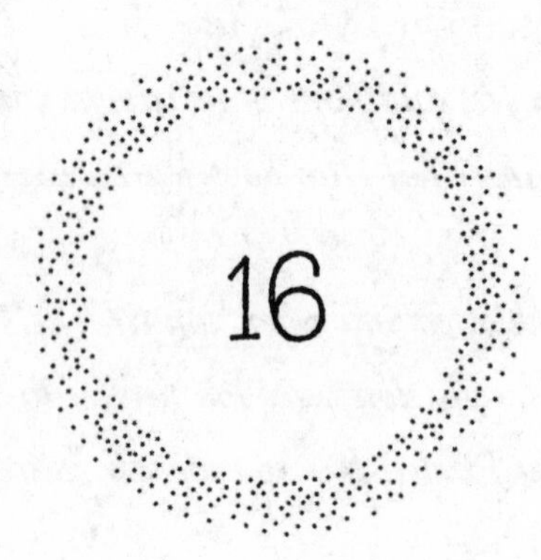

APRIL, FOUR YEARS AGO

Eight years old

Four years and four months before Jade eavesdropped on my plan, Dr. Leo Lacamoire was being honored at MIT with a Distinguished Professor award. He wore a tuxedo to the ceremony. He had made a breakthrough in new planetary discoveries this year, and although his past mistakes—and oh, he had made them!—clung to his memory, he could easily shove them out of his mind. He didn't yet know that his Star-Gazer Twelve, stolen from him years before, was buried underground in Moose Junction, Wisconsin.

He didn't know that the thief was dying.

But we aren't at that part of the story yet. The story where I learn just how the Star-Gazer Twelve got from Dr. Leo Lacamoire's observatory in Cambridge, Massachusetts, to a box in a tourist town. No, I'm only eight years old. I'm a third grader, learning how to add three-digit numbers and make connections from books to my own experience. Dad and I go to the park almost every night to look through his telescope.

Blair goes to the Sweet Toes Ballet School in Cedar Valley. She's fourteen years old, and by far the best in her class. Everyone says so.

Their spring recital was boring. I almost fell asleep. You always think ballet is over, and then it keeps going and going and going. Mom let me bring Sophie, and we spent most of the night writing notes back and forth and giggling. When it was time for Blair to dance, we all sat still as stone. She was dynamite, as usual. I wished I was as good at something as Blair was at ballet, but I was pretty average in every way you could think of. I got good grades, and I could read quickly, but I couldn't dance or draw or play sports. Jade bought Sophie and me candy with her own allowance money at intermission. We went downstairs and checked out the fancy bathrooms. Blair was usually busy now, taking ballet five nights a week, but Jade still looked out for me.

Afterward, we were in the parking lot getting ready to go. Blair was with us, but she was just coming home to shower before going to sleep over at her friend Elisha's house. A man ran up to our family, his nose delicately pointed in the air, his wrinkly hands holding out a card.

"I own the most superior dance studio in the Midwest," he said stiffly. "My studio's in Milwaukee. Auditions are over, but for a dancer of your caliber, I suppose I could open a spot. Is she homeschooled?"

"What?" asked Dad.

"Homeschooled," he said impatiently. "Do you go to school? Most dancers in the Aleksander Alekseev's Milwaukee School for Classical Ballet devote half of their day to ballet."

"School? She has to go to school," Dad said.

But what my mom said, in a soft voice was, "Company? You want her to dance on a company team?"

And that was how Blair was put on the path to stardom. Because we didn't get into the car fast enough.

We didn't know, then. We couldn't see. And that's the story of the universe, pretty much—guessing, fumbling around in the dark. Trying to figure out what happens next. Doing the best you can with the information that you have, until you learn more.

It would be easy to blame ballet, or Aleksander. My mom does. But I think there was something in Blair that whole time. Anna Rexia was always there, like a little seed, waiting to be watered. Sure, Aleksander Alekseev's Milwaukee School for Classical Ballet handed it to her. But Blair was the one who listened.

That night, Dad and I looked at the stars through my telescope.

"It's mind-boggling how far away they are," he said. "They feel so close, like we could reach out and touch them, don't they?"

But they weren't. You could fly for hours and hours, years and years, and not even come close to some of those stars. They looked small enough to fit in your pocket, but they were actually gigantic.

It's crazy, really, how different things are from how they look.

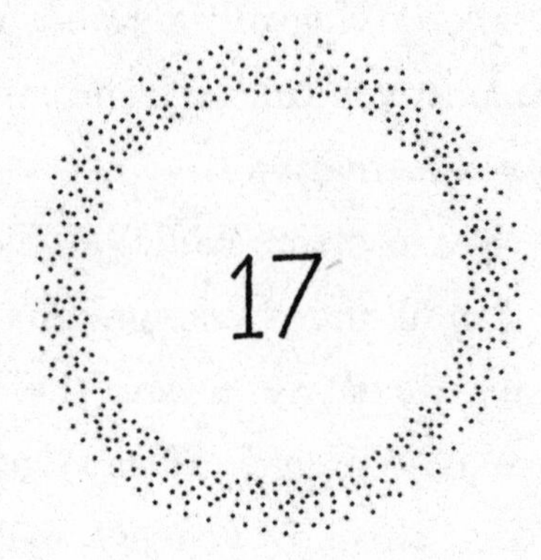

AUGUST, PRESENT DAY

Twelve years old

The morning of the eclipse, I woke up early. I could hear Mom running around downstairs, throwing a pile of laundry in the wash and tripping over Obi's bowl of food.

When I got to the living room, Dad was already watching the news. He stood behind the couch, bouncing on the balls of his feet. It was so bizarre to see Main Street in the background of every major news channel. There were journalists from the *Today* show standing in front of Java Jane's. I saw Harrison in the background, his very own ten seconds of fame. Jade was parked at the kitchen table eating cereal.

"Hey, kiddo!" said Dad. "Today's the big day! I thought we'd head over around twelve o'clock. Make sure we get prime seating!"

"The eclipse is happening in the sky," said Jade, rolling her eyes. "It's not like you're going to miss it."

"What are you even doing awake?" I asked.

She shrugged, looking right at me. "Couldn't sleep."

A lie can affect everyone around you, and mine was like the beating heart in that freaky poem we had read in school. It pounded under the floorboards and kept the whole room awake. It was becoming best friends with Anna Rexia, haunting the house.

My plan was to go downtown with Dad, check out the festival, and then tell him I had to go quickly say hi to Sophie. I would disappear, then claim the crowds had been so packed I hadn't been able to find my way back. He would be totally disappointed, but I couldn't think of anything else to do. I had told Leo and Simone I'd be digging during the eclipse, when everyone was occupied. I had hidden a shovel the night before, tucked under the bench in front of the library.

It was far from a foolproof plan, but it was the best thing I had.

"I have to go run an errand," said Mom. "But I'll be

back in time for the big event."

"Where are you going?" I asked, surprised. "Aren't you coming with us?"

"Traffic is gonna suck," Jade pointed out.

She bopped Jade on the head with a dish towel. "A guest was driving back from Washport this morning and they're having car trouble. I've got to go give them a jump. I'll be back, don't you worry."

I spent the rest of the morning being lazy and watching pre-eclipse coverage with Dad while Jade sat on her phone. All I did was wait, wait, wait, staring at the clock.

Main Street was *packed*. You could barely move through the crowds. Disappearing was going to be easier than I thought. All the shop owners had tables out front, and news vans lined the side of the road. Coontail's had huge buckets of mini sunscreens and bottles of water, sweating in the heat. Everywhere you looked, there were lawn chairs and excited tourists. Loud music played out of speakers and it was hot enough that people were running around in swimsuits. Almost everyone I knew was there, on one single street.

I imagined what we would have been doing if Blair was here. She would have been so excited, picking out the best viewing spot, sketching Captain Moonbeard sailing across the sky in front of the moon. I wondered if she'd be watching from the front lawn at Harvest Hills.

I'm doing this for Blair, I reminded myself as I looked at my dad. If he knew why I had to do it, he would understand.

But was I doing it for Blair? Or was I doing it for me? Or for Dr. Leo Lacamoire? The reasons swirled together, mixing with all the inevitable bumps in the road and people who could get hurt. All I knew was that I had to do this. Sometimes you just keep saying yes and you don't even know why.

That telescope was being returned, and it was being returned today.

Dad and I walked around for a little bit, just taking it all in. I glanced at my phone. The eclipse was starting in only thirty minutes. I had to get moving.

"Harriet!" She was sitting outside of Java Jane's at a card table, with a handmade banner reading *Save the Library* draped across the front.

"Hey, Abby," she said. "This is perfect, isn't it? I've been in the background of, like, four news cameras so far. Maybe if we got some national publicity, people could start sending in some dollar bills. Lord, it's hot out here." She fanned herself with her clipboard.

"That's awesome," I said. "Are you getting lots of signatures?"

"Tons," she said.

I said goodbye and Dad gave me a Look. The Look clearly said: Poor Harriet. Keep your expectations nice and low. That library is going down, signatures or not.

It was hard, though, not to feel hopeful just then. The energy on Main Street made the entire town feel electric. Everyone's eyes were upward, toward the sky, wondering, *When? How? What will it be like?* You couldn't *not* feel hopeful, in a place like that. I understood Leo just then—knowing the truth about hope's frailty but placing all his bets on it anyway. Because what, really, was the alternative?

Someone grabbed my arm. When I whipped around, I was surprised—it was Simone. Our plan had been to avoid each other all day. We didn't want to cause any suspicion. Leo's paranoia had worn off on me.

"He wants to go," she said through her teeth. I glanced over at my dad, who was chatting excitedly with Harrison.

"*What?*"

"Leo. He wants to be there when you dig the stupid thing up. I swear to God, this is the last crazy thing I do for this man. I'm quitting in the morning. But until then, I'm under strict orders to grab you and bring you to the library."

"I'm riding my bike!" I insisted.

"Not anymore."

"He can't come," I said, almost out of breath. "The CNN interview. The *alibi* . . ."

"He doesn't care. Oh, Abby, he's lost his mind," said Simone, shaking her head. "He wants this telescope so badly. He wants it the second it's dug up. He's skipping the CNN thing, and he wants to be with you when it happens. There's no talking sense to him."

Crap. This was not the plan. I shook my head. "No," I said. "Simone! He can't be there. Telescope goes missing, famous astronomer, hello?"

"I can't. I *tried*."

"Then you don't need me," I said desperately. "Dig it up on your own."

"He wants you there. You've helped us so much. This is your thing, too. He wants to do it together, so you get a chance to see it."

I put my face in my hands. Suddenly, I saw: I didn't want to rescue that stupid telescope. I didn't want an introduction to Joanna Creech. I wanted this whole thing to disappear. I couldn't do this. The determination that I had felt so strongly only a minute ago had sailed away like a tourist on a boat, flying off across Fishtrap Lake into the sunset.

"There's only one shovel," I said desperately, my last-ditch attempt.

"Abby," said Simone, grabbing my wrists. Her hands were sweaty. "I know we're asking you to do something ridiculous. But—Leo has been through so much. He is so, so desperate. I am begging you to help me out on this."

Harriet's face flashed through my mind. Oh, this is why you don't lie! The tangled web, Mr. Linn had quoted in English. That stupid tangled web *I* had woven.

But what could I say? There she was.

"Dad," I said, turning around. "Dad!" He had been talking with Harrison and his kids about which setting on their iPhones would take better eclipse photos, but now he turned to look at me. "I have to go somewhere. I'll be right back."

"What? Where on earth could you have to go?" We were practically yelling to each other over the noise.

"I forgot my eclipse glasses."

"Abigail! How could you? But I'm sure we could buy some around here . . . or you can just look through mine."

I shook my head. "No. I need those specific ones. I'll be right back. Simone can drive me."

"My car's only a street over," she told Dad.

"Abby, geez! Run like the wind," said Dad. "Traffic is going to be horrible. Hurry! You can't miss this. It's what we've been *waiting* for."

Simone and I raced to her car, not one street over, but a solid three blocks. We hopped in and she slammed on the gas, weaving in and out of tourists looking for parking spots. I held on for dear life.

We stopped at Eagle's Nest, and Dr. Leo Lacamoire came outside, looking terrified. I was about to learn so much. So many questions were going to be answered. But in that exact moment, all that I saw was a scared, sad old man—nothing like the man in the TED Talk. This one didn't look like he could find his shoes, let alone a new planet.

He got in the car, slamming the door.

My phone buzzed. It was Dad—*where ru?*

"Maybe I shouldn't do this," I said weakly. "I promised my dad I would watch this with him ages ago. It's, like, our special thing . . . if *you're* going to dig it up, you don't need *me*."

Leo waved something in front of my face. I looked a

little closer—it was a business card. Joanna Creech.

"Just like I promised," he said. "She owes me; I've made her piles of money. You helped us find where it was, now you'll help us get it out. I'm an old man and my back isn't what it used to be."

There was no getting out of this.

We sped down the road to the library, bypassing Main Street. There was the crowd of people, and among the miles of tourists, I saw a few familiar faces. Miss Mae, in a shiny American flag T-shirt. Joe from Hank's Hardware and More, giving someone directions. My own parents. And—

A flash of brown hair, the same shade as mine.

Could it be?

"Stop the car!" I yelled.

"We can't. No time," said Simone, eyes straight ahead as we sailed over a pothole. "This thing starts in fifteen minutes."

My eyes must have been playing tricks on me. I craned my neck, trying to see Main Street better as we whizzed by. But I could have sworn I had seen—

"We're almost there," said Leo, bouncing in his seat like a toddler about to get a Happy Meal.

When we pulled in front of the library, I was

right—there was nobody there. Uselman Road was completely deserted.

We got out of the car and hurried over to the spot on the corner of the property. Simone dragged the shovel behind her, but when we got there, she handed it to me.

"You do the honors," she said. "That was the plan."

Think, Abby! Think! But I did the only thing I could do—I started digging. Simone and Leo stood there, antsy, looking around. It was already getting much darker as the moon and the sun met in the same place. It was as if the sun was setting in rapid speed. I wanted to look, but I didn't want to burn my eyeballs off. Leo offered to help dig and let me look through his glasses, but I shook my head. I had to do this. I couldn't just be standing there when he learned the truth.

"CNN has sent eight emails," said Simone, shielding her eyes and flipping through her phone.

"CNN will be fine," said Leo, practically shaking.

I dug and dug and dug, my arms burning, until the shovel went *pling* against something metal.

"That's it!" said Leo, his voice sounding wild. "That's it!"

I dug around the edges, trying to find a way to wiggle the box out. It seemed big. No, it was *huge*, half the size of my refrigerator and way too heavy for us to get up. Yet another hole in the World's Worst Plan. We bent down and tried pulling it. We got it about halfway aboveground, yanking and grunting with all our might as the sun set above us. Dust and dirt fell on the lawn, covering my legs. I looked like I had been cave diving or something. The thing was super heavy; I dug a little more on the sides.

"Your back, Leo. Stop," said Simone.

But she and I couldn't get it out—we were a grad student who loved Shakespeare and a twelve-year-old liar. Not exactly power lifters. We needed all the help we could get, even if it was from a scientist with an achy back.

"Good thing we came," panted Simone. "What were we thinking? You'd never be able to get this out alone. Science Genius and Literature Dork need a Common Sense 101 class."

"We'll never be able to get it out *together*," I said, hoping desperately that I was right and that that box would stay buried where it belonged.

We only had it up halfway, but Leo, in a stroke of unfortunate brilliance, just leaned down and heaved the top off.

"We should have thought of that," hissed Simone,

smacking herself in the forehead. "Duh."

Leaning down, they started pulling out items. Baseball cards. A Bible. But no telescope.

"No," he whispered. "*No.*"

It wasn't there.

I *knew* it wouldn't be there.

And that was the lie.

Because I knew exactly where that telescope was. And I knew it wasn't in that hole.

"Leo," I whispered.

He shook his head. He was practically shaking. "But—but that picture. And she swore! She *swore* this is where she put it!" He put his head in his hands.

"Leo," I said louder. "I . . ."

Simone put her hand on my arm. "Not now, Abby," she said quietly. The sun was completely blocked and we stood in darkness. It was incredible, like the middle of the night in the middle of the day. Some confused birds started chirping, and we heard a dull roar come from Main Street. Here it was, the moment I'd been waiting for all summer. Here it was, the moment I could tell the truth.

Tears started to poke behind my eyes, and no matter how hard I blinked, I couldn't get rid of them. I wished I could go back to when Dr. Leo Lacamoire had first told me about the telescope. No, I wished I could go back to the night I first saw him, when I wished for adventure and the stupid universe gave me exactly what I'd asked for. I would tell the truth this time. I would.

But we couldn't go back—none of us could. Not me, not Blair, not Dr. Leo Lacamoire, PhD.

"Leo. I know where it is," I said, choking out a sob. "The telescope . . ."

A car door slammed and we all jumped.

"Who is it?" called out Simone, practically shaking. "Crap," she muttered. "Crap, crap, crap."

"Abby?"

And there was Jade. My sister, holding a heavy black case—the same case she had taken from under my bed while Simone and I were picking up Leo. That case had not been underground. It had been in my very own house, in my very own room, waiting to be revealed. The center of that tangled web was inside, being lugged this very minute by the sister I had thought hated me.

Dr. Leo Lacamoire looked at me. Then back to the case. Then back at me. His eyes were confused.

"What's going on, Abby?" he asked. Simone was staring, too.

“I’m sorry,” I said, my voice cracking. I was going to cry.

“I tried to hurry,” Jade said, her own voice wobbling. “I thought I could beat you here. I thought—”

I shook my head. This wasn’t Jade’s fault. She dragged the case over, unsure of what to do with it, before deciding to just lay it at my feet. I opened the clunky silver clasps, and there it was—the Star-Gazer Twelve, lying in red velvet.

Just as it had been when I stole it five years ago.

Simone looked at me, completely confused.

“What on earth is going on? Where did that come from?” asked Simone.

But Leo didn’t even care. He reached for it, and before I knew what he was doing, he picked up the heavy scope and unscrewed the focuser. He shook it, and out fell a small, rolled-up piece of paper. He unrolled it. It was a picture—a super faded one—of a young Dr. Leo Lacamoire, and a little girl. They were pressed cheek to cheek, laughing.

Then the great Dr. Leo Lacamoire, PhD, world-renowned scientist, bent his head and began to cry.

And the sun began to shine again.

AUGUST, FIVE YEARS AGO

Seven years old

Five years before I dug up that time capsule for the *sec-ond* time, when the middle of the day turned as dark as the night, I was seven years old.

A summer of being seven means sunshine and library books and the freedom of days with no responsibilities. My sisters were eleven and thirteen, both older and younger than I was the summer of Dr. Leo Lacamoire. We did everything together when Blair wasn't at dance and Jade wasn't at piano lessons, which she still took back then. They were my best friends.

I didn't have a ton of other people to hang around.

Sophie had gone to spend the summer with her grandparents in Denver, and Lex still lived in Minneapolis. All I had was Blair and Jade, really, and all they had was me, because our town was tiny and neither of them could drive yet. But that was fine. They were all I needed. I would have chosen them, anyway. Blair was our fearless leader, throwing down dares and trying to be the bravest. Jade was fierce, flighty, funny, always making us laugh. And me? I was just along for the ride.

One day, we were at the library. We were almost always at the library. Blair liked to read comics, Jade always chose books about girls her own age going to normal schools and having normal problems, and I would read pretty much anything. We would pick out books and bring them by the bagful to the dock, where we'd smear on sunscreen and peel clementines and read for hours.

"Nice shirt," someone snorted. I turned and saw a boy a little older than me; maybe Jade's age.

I looked down. I had a Stormtrooper on my shirt. So what?

"Thanks . . . ," I said nervously.

He rolled his eyes. "Bet you don't even know the difference between a clone trooper and a Stormtrooper."

My face got hot. *I do, too,* I wanted to yell.

"Girls don't know anything about Star Wars," he said. "Do you even know what Luke's home planet is?"

Tatooine.

"Or who Ahsoka is?"

Anakin's Padawan.

"Or who became the first chancellor of the New Republic?"

"Mon Mothma," a voice snapped. It was Blair, with her hands on her hips. She glared at the boy.

He rolled his eyes and turned around to leave, but not before Jade walked over.

"Hey," she said. "Are you being a jerk to my sisters?"

"No," he muttered.

"Good," said Jade. "Because I'd hate to have an *issue*." Jade had no idea what a Padawan *was*, let alone who had been Anakin's, but she was the only one allowed to tease me and Blair, and everyone knew it.

If someone had talked to me like that, I would have burst into tears. But he grumbled something under his breath and left, chasing after his parents. My face was still hot. I felt like I was going to cry.

"Abby," said Jade, shaking her head. "You have to stand up for yourself. You can't just let people be jerks like that."

Blair snickered. "Did you see his face when Jade laid into him?"

Jade flipped her hair. "Ooh, big tough guy, picking on a little kid. What*ever*." She made a face, mimicking his wide eyes, and Blair and I cracked up.

"Me bully," Jade groaned like a caveman, stomping around. "Me Star Wars expert. Me eat little girls for breakfast."

Harriet walked over, her hands overflowing with books. "You girls," she said. "I heard that little runt. What an idiot." Were adults allowed to call kids idiots? Harriet did whatever she wanted.

"You all right, Abby?" I nodded, feeling better. Blair and Jade were like my own superhero cape. You couldn't mess with me without messing with them. I didn't need to be tough. I had them. And they were always there, a million times stronger than I was.

"Well, I know something that might cheer you up," she said quietly. "I know a secret."

"What?" asked Blair excitedly. Summer days were all starting to look the same. We wanted adventure. We wanted a *quest*. A *secret*, whispered to us by Harriet, one that would transform our day into an epic battle. We wanted to be like girls in books, ones with voyages to go on. We wanted to be larger than we were.

That's when Harriet told us about the telescope buried outside. She had just stumbled upon the archives while helping Waukegan County scan them to the library database, and she knew I loved everything about outer space. Even though Jade couldn't have cared less about the stars, it was still exciting—a telescope worth a gazillion dollars, buried underground? A hidden time capsule right here in Moose Junction?

I wanted that telescope. It was all I could think about for days. When Blair came into my and Jade's room one morning, we knew instantly she had a mission. She was holding a bowl of cereal, but she hadn't even touched it.

"I say we dig it up," she said.

"Dig what up?" Jade rubbed the sleep from her eyes. She had already forgotten.

"The Star-Gazer Twelve. The telescope! It doesn't deserve to be buried underground. It should be used," she said.

"First of all, it's a telescope, not a lost puppy. Second of all, we can't dig it up! Are you crazy? It's a time capsule. It's supposed to stay buried," said Jade. "We'd probably go to jail or something."

Blair shrugged, turning around.

Then she made some chicken noises. The sisterly kiss of death.

Jade threw a pillow at her, bawking right back, and that's when I knew—we were digging up that time capsule.

That night was the perfect time to do it. Mom and Dad were going into Washport with some friends, and we had rented a movie and ordered pizza. Blair was thirteen, old enough to babysit us. We waved goodbye, promising to lock the doors, knowing they wouldn't be home till late. They didn't go out often, but when they did, they made the most of it.

We all rode our bikes to the library. It was the most exhilarating thing I had ever felt. It was pitch-black outside, and we were in thick sweatshirts. I was practically shaking I was so nervous, but Blair and Jade were just laughing. They weren't nervous at all. They would have walked through fire and dared it to burn them. They were *made* for voyages.

When we got there, we dug up the time capsule. Harriet had told us right where it was, and Blair had brought a shovel from the garage. She did most of the digging—she was so strong from ballet back then, when food meant *fuel* and *muscle* and *endurance*—while Jade cleared away rocks and dirt. I kept a lookout. When the shovel hit the case, we realized how big it was—that sinking realization Simone and Leo had had, that this box was not a shoebox but a heavy metal thing that five strong townspeople had had to lower into the ground in 2000. Jade had been the one who reached down and simply yanked the top off. That's when we saw it—there was the telescope, in its heavy black case. We opened it up and just stared at it.

"Holy crap," Blair breathed. "This is awesome. I can't wait to try it out."

"Try it out? I thought we were just looking at it," I said.

She laughed. "No way! This thing is ours now. No one will ever know. Besides Harriet. It's our secret." A secret, like a pact—like a promise that would tie us together. Blair and Jade and me. The three of us braided together over this amazing thing we had discovered.

We did take it home, but we couldn't even figure out how to put it together. It didn't matter—the fun part had been discovering it, and reburying the time capsule. Nobody even noticed the lump of dirt, and if they had, they wouldn't have cared. It was Moose Junction. I'd explained that to Dr. Leo Lacamoire and Simone, but they didn't get it. People here saw a lump of dirt, they assumed it was just a lump of dirt.

I kept the Star-Gazer Twelve under my bed. Blair probably forgot about it. I was almost positive Jade had. Even I forgot about it most days. But once in a while, I would lug it out and run my hand over it. I never did figure out how to put the parts together, and besides, I couldn't risk Mom and Dad bursting in and noticing a telescope that definitely wasn't mine. Instead, I would just admire it, in its weather-protectant case that had kept it safe all these years. I would remember a time when everything was perfect.

I've had it ever since.

I am a liar, remember? I told you that, way back on page one. It's not my fault you didn't listen. You should trust people when they tell you what they are. You should believe them when they are admitting their own smallness.

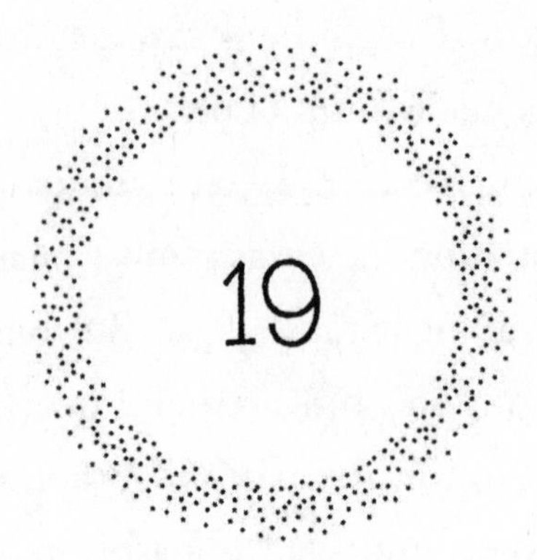

Once upon a time, there was a brilliant scientist named Dr. Leo Lacamoire.

Leo found new planets and studied the ones we already knew. He made maps of the stars. He knew everything about the moon. He once went to the White House to advocate for the space program.

This scientific genius was madly in love with a woman named Trish. Trish was from Wisconsin, and she was a journalist. She interviewed Dr. Leo Lacamoire for *Time* magazine, and he told her that her eyes were more beautiful than all the stars in the sky combined. (Simone rolled her eyes at that part, but I thought it was nice.)

Dr. Leo Lacamoire and Trish didn't get married, though, because they traveled too much. Leo was always giving talks in places like Beijing and Venice and London, and Trish was busy traveling around the world to write stories for publications. But whenever they could meet up, they did. Leo wrote her love poems and sent her roses, and Trish said that if he stopped traveling and settled down, she would, too. But the only thing Leo loved more than Trish was space, and you couldn't study space in one place. You had to go find it.

Trish and Leo ended up having a baby. Trish pleaded for him to quit traveling the world and spending time looking up at the stars and instead just take care of her and the baby. But the truth was, even though Leo loved Trish and the baby very much, he was blinded by his work. ("Like you can be blinded by the sun," I said. "Exactly," Simone smiled back.)

Over time, that baby grew and grew. Dr. Leo Lacamoire always sent her nice birthday presents and called her on Christmas and saw her when he could, but he was becoming more and more famous. Then MIT asked him to be a professor. Trish thought finally, she and the baby could move out to Massachusetts and they could be a family. But the world-renowned scientist told her not to. He wasn't in love with her anymore, even though he still *loved* her. ("That's the dumbest thing I've ever heard," I sighed. "You're telling me," said Simone.)

Trish was heartbroken, but so was the baby, who was now not a baby at all but actually a little girl. Trish pointed Dr. Leo Lacamoire out to the girl when he would be on TV, but slowly he called less and less, and he never went to visit them anymore. He still sent presents on her birthday, but that little girl started to not like her dad so much. Because what kind of dad has time to find new planets but doesn't have time to find McFarland, Wisconsin? No kind of dad.

So that little girl grew and grew, watching her dad on TV, but getting really mad at him. One day, when she was seventeen years old, she went out east to look at colleges with her mom. She asked her dad if they could get lunch. She was going to tell him everything she thought—that he had been a bad dad her whole life, and that she didn't understand why he acted that way, but that she loved him and wanted to give him another chance. They met up in his office, but after she'd been there for less than a minute, someone knocked on door. The *New York Times* was on the phone and needed a quote about some new black hole images. Dr. Leo Lacamoire left, and the little girl—not a little girl anymore, a teenage girl—had to wait and wait and wait. And while she waited, she got even angrier. Because she was being very nice giving him a chance, and he was taking advantage of her. So she saw a fancy telescope behind his desk, and a case next to it, and she just snapped. She stole that telescope and ran out the door.

Dr. Leo Lacamoire called her and called her, but she wouldn't answer the phone. She waited for the cops to show up at her door and demand the telescope back, but they never did.

Every summer, she and Trish went to a town called Moose Junction for a week. That summer was going to be the town's hundredth-birthday celebration, one that would include the creation of a time capsule, she'd heard. And that's when Lyra Lacamoire had an idea: an idea that snuck into her heart and spun a web around a secret.

She hated that stupid telescope. Every time she looked at it, she thought of her mean dad who loved his newsletter subscribers more than he loved her. And so when the town created the time capsule that summer, she did the most horrible thing she could think of—she buried that telescope right down in it, so that nobody could ever find it. It would never be used—it would gather dust, buried deep in the ground.

Eighteen years later, that little girl was thirty-five years old. She had not talked to her dad since. But she was very, very sick. She had lung cancer, even though she'd never smoked one cigarette. She was thinking about her life and her greatest mistake: stealing that telescope from a man who simply didn't know how to love people the way he loved planets. She called her father, who had been trying to track her down for years, and told him everything.

But Dr. Leo Lacamoire, PhD, had learned so much in those years, and not just about gamma-ray bursts. He had seen so much of the galaxy that he had begun to feel small: so small, like a dot in the huge landscape of the world. He had thought that the more he knew, the more important he would become, but with all the speeches and awards and TV appearances, he had realized that the opposite was true. The more he knew, the sadder he was. He was no longer Leo, the guy who loved the stars and research and a pretty girl from Wisconsin. He was Dr. Lacamoire, and that person felt entirely different. When he filmed his Netflix special, he came home at night to a sad, empty hotel room and had vending machine candy for dinner. That can make anyone reevaluate their life choices.

And he was so thrilled to hear from his daughter that he wasn't even mad about the telescope. When he learned she was dying, he was devastated. He got on an airplane and flew to Wisconsin as fast as he could, but he was too late—his daughter had died. ("Where was Trish?" I asked. "Traveling Europe," said Simone. "She worked in Paris as a correspondent for the *Washington Post.* It all happened so fast. Nobody knew she had such little time left.")

Dr. Leo Lacamoire was in despair. But the woman—Lyra Lacamoire, his daughter he loved more than anything even though he didn't know how to show it—had left him a letter, telling him where he could find his telescope and apologizing for everything. Of course, it was Leo who needed to apologize, and even though he was able to do so on the phone, it wasn't enough. He had let an opportunity pass him by—to not just be beloved by science, but to be beloved by a family. And little did Lyra Lacamoire know that it wasn't the telescope he longed for, it was what was inside it—a photograph of the two of them together, taken when she was a very little girl and he still visited her sometimes, folded up and stuck in the focus finder. That was what he had been so upset to lose.

He knew he had to get the telescope—it was the only thing left of his daughter. So he hatched a plan to travel to Moose Junction, Wisconsin, and dig up the time capsule himself. He would never see Lyra again. He would never turn back time. But he could retrieve that telescope, and the picture inside it. This, at least, he could do.

"He'll never speak to me again," I said to Simone, who had spilled this entire story to Jade and me as we sat on the curb. Dr. Leo Lacamoire had taken the photograph of him and Lyra and driven off in the car, ignoring Simone's pleas. He wouldn't even so much as look at me. "I had it this whole time. I just . . ." I shrugged. "It was kind of like my own photograph."

"We dug it up with our sister," said Jade. "And she's really sick. She might not ever get better."

Simone nodded. "I know. I understand. It was wrong to lie to us, but I do understand. Leo will, too, eventually. That old man has been through the wringer. He'll heal from this."

We sat there, right on the curb, and I realized I didn't give a single crap who saw us in front of the dug-up time capsule. I mean, really, who was going to get mad? Harriet? I highly doubted I would be hearing from Joanna Creech now. Officer J.J. could come drag me off in handcuffs for vandalizing public property for all I cared. He was probably too busy directing traffic off Main Street. I almost laughed at how stupid and foolish this whole thing had been. All this work for a box that had been under my bed. I was tired of hiding and lying. I sat there in the sunlight and dared to let the whole world see what I'd done. But nobody drove by. That part of the plan, at least, had worked.

"That's so sad, about Dr. Lacamoire," said Jade. "He could have been with his daughter for thirty-five years, but instead he just let her live her own life. He missed so much."

Simone nodded. "It's the saddest thing in the world. It truly is."

It was sad, but not the saddest thing in the world. I didn't say that, but I thought it. The saddest thing in the world would be if he never had a chance to apologize. The saddest thing in the world would be if all hope was lost. At least he got the chance to say sorry.

I knew exactly why Dr. Leo Lacamoire didn't call Lyra sooner. Because what if he did and she never forgave him?

What if he said sorry and she hung up the phone? The saddest thing in the world was to live frozen, because you were so unsure of what would happen next.

But he had not done that. He had plunged forward. He had *tried*, and he had that to hold on to.

"I'm not much for science," said Simone, "but Leo told me something pretty interesting once."

"What?" asked Jade. I wasn't even listening. I was staring off into space, the infinite nothingness that had stolen Leo from his family. Simone put her arms around us.

"The atoms that make us up—you and me and Lyra and Leo and even Obi—are the same atoms that once made up stars," said Simone. "When stars explode, they send atoms all over the galaxy. Those atoms are like little seeds that form new galaxies. They form *us*. We're all made of stardust." She leaned back and held her hand up to her eyes, staring straight at the sun.

"That makes me feel tiny," said Jade.

"Little specks," I said absentmindedly. But Simone shook her head.

"No," she said softly. "Don't you see? It makes me feel huge. We *are* huge. We're part of this sky, but this sky is also part of us."

AUGUST, PRESENT DAY

Twelve years old

The eclipse was over. All that buildup for a couple of minutes of darkness. But it had been something spectacular, right here in Moose Junction. That I would not forget.

Leo had taken Simone's car, but she said she could walk back to Eagle's Nest when Jade offered her a ride.

"It's far!" I protested. "Three miles, at least . . ."

"I need some fresh air anyway," Simone said. I had a feeling she wasn't excited to get back to Leo.

"You girls," she said, giving us each a hug. "It'll be okay, all right? Everything will be just fine. You get back to your parents now."

Jade nodded toward the beat-up Toyota. It had been Blair's; the *I'd Rather Be Dancing* bumper sticker was just starting to peel off in the corners. The stupid thing had stubbornly stayed on ever since Blair got her license. It seemed perfect, suddenly, to be hopping into Blair's car. It was like she was there with us. The three McCourt sisters, returning that telescope so long after we took it. Jade and I rode in silence for a minute before I opened my mouth.

"Thanks," I said.

She didn't answer.

"You didn't have to do that," I continued. "I could have . . . I don't know. Figured something out."

I couldn't see her face, and we rode quietly for another couple of minutes before she spoke up.

"I was worried about you," she said. "I didn't know what you were going to do."

"I thought you forgot about the telescope," I told her.

"How could I ever forget that?" she asked. "You think I could *forget* that?"

I had been wrong about so many things. I had been so stupid! Jade, Sophie—people I had thought were gone forever weren't. The stars I thought were dead were still shining. You could undo a lie, if you tried hard enough.

"Why didn't you tell them right away?" asked Jade.

The easy answer was that I was afraid of getting in trouble. Was stealing something buried really *stealing*? Can you be put in jail for something you did when you were seven? I didn't know, but I also didn't want to find out.

But there was another answer hiding under that answer, the same as that chocolate cream hiding in a doughnut. The telescope: it reminded me of sisters and secrets and magic, of a time when things were perfect. It was mine.

That was the truth. But there was another truth, too: the truth of who that telescope belonged to. It was time for the Star-Gazer Twelve to go home.

"I don't know," I said honestly.

"What was your plan if I didn't get there?" asked Jade. "Just let him dig and find nothing?"

"I was going to move some dirt around and then just drop the telescope at Eagle's Nest," I said. "I was supposed to be *alone*. I wasn't expecting him to want to *come*."

"Stick to astronomy, Abby. I think your short-lived career as a secret agent was a bust."

The traffic was still clogged up. We found a parking spot a couple of streets away from the viewing party, zipping into a spot as an exhausted-looking woman in a pickup truck pulled out. Jade and I hustled to Main Street and pushed our way through the crowds, looking everywhere for our parents. *A New Hope* was going to be played over the projector soon, and all the lawn chairs had been replaced with blankets. Miss Mae was selling popcorn from a stand. I'd never seen so many people in our town in my life. I ran into Sophie's mom, who wrapped me into a hug and asked me how Blair was doing.

"Abby!"

It was Jade, calling to me. She waved me over from across the crowd. She had a huge smile on her face. I headed toward her, shoving through tourists and locals and journalists alike.

"That was something, wasn't it, Abby?" said Father Peter Patrick, patting my shoulder as I walked by. "God's creation is outstanding."

"*Abby.*" Another voice. One that was all too familiar. One I'd know anywhere.

It couldn't be. But there she was.

Blair.

Standing right there, in a Green Bay Packers sweatshirt and ripped denim shorts, her hair in a tight ponytail.

"Abby." She had yelled my name a million times—

across the dock, from her bedroom, on a thousand and one car trips to the Ice Shanty. Over her shoulder, yelling at me to follow her. The night we dug the telescope, telling me to keep watch. And I hadn't heard it from her all summer.

"Abby," she said a third time. She was smiling—a *real* smile, one that met her eyes—and opened her arms wide. Wide enough for both Jade and me. And as the three of us pressed together, I knew that whatever happened next, the power of three would not be broken. We were bound together—not by any secret, but by the sky itself.

We sat out on a dock, feet dangling. Blair and I looked across the lake, listening to Caleb's band play bad covers.

"You're back," I said.

"I'm back," she said. "You missed my graduation ceremony. Caps and gowns and everything."

"Really?"

"*No*," she laughed. "Just a hug from my roommate and some meds and an outpatient therapist to see in Washport."

Blair was still skinny, but she looked more rounded out. The nooks and crannies of her knees and shoulders had been filled, and her skin had a bit of its shine back. I could hug her without feeling like she'd break.

"I missed you," I said.

"I missed *you*."

"I've missed you for a long time," I said honestly. Longer than the summer; longer than the past year, even. She knew what I meant.

"You know why I went to Harvest Hills?" she asked, watching an eagle swoop down and snatch something out of the water.

"To get better," I said.

She nodded. "Yeah. But I went because of you. The Joffrey thing, my accident on prom night, the cupcake . . ." She squeezed her eyes shut and shook her head, her brown ponytail grazing my face. "All I could think about was how you had seen me make really stupid decisions."

"You were sick," I said.

"I know! I *know* that. But still. I didn't want you to see that and think that was how things should be," she said. "I always felt like maybe . . . like you looked up to me. And this was one thing I didn't want you to look up to. I saw you, after the Memorial Day . . . thing. I saw your face when Mom and I got in the car. And you looked like someone had just told you everything you'd ever believed was a lie. Confused. And scared."

I nodded. "I was. My whole life, you'd been so perfect. And suddenly it was like maybe I'd never even known you."

"You know me," said Blair, her voice getting tight. "You know who I am without ballet. That's something I'm still kinda figuring out." She shifted, stretching her arms and arching her back to the sky. In that moment, she looked a little like the ballerina she'd always been.

"Dad's gonna kill you for missing the eclipse," she said. "They were looking everywhere. Where *were* you?"

But before I could answer, we heard someone call out.

"Hey." We turned and saw Jade walking toward us slowly. "You two having Secret Sister Nerd Time or something?"

Blair opened her mouth with a retort, and it was like nothing had changed. But so much had. So instead, I scooted over, probably getting a thousand splinters in my butt from the wooden dock, and patted the space I'd left.

It was just an invitation. I had no idea if she'd accept. But she did, coming over, plopping down next to me. She slid into her own place in our complicated dance. She told Blair she was glad she was home, and Blair smiled.

It wasn't perfect, not by a long shot. But it felt a bit like unburying that time capsule: excavating the dirt and feeling the sun come back out.

That night, as I watched Luke blow up the Death Star between my two sisters, with Blair quoting the lines and Jade rolling her eyes, I didn't know what was to come. I was pretty convinced I would never speak to Dr. Leo Lacamoire again. He was gone, like a shooting star streaking across the galaxy. He had found what he wanted and was furious with me for not telling him that I'd had it. I got that. He and Simone left early the next morning. Simone stopped over to say goodbye to my mom and return the keys, but afterward, she gave me a long hug.

"He just needs some time," she whispered into my ear. "We'll be in touch, all right, stargazer?"

Over the next year, as I forged my way through eighth grade, I did hear from Leo. Twice, but not actually directly from him. In September, an anonymous donor wrote a huge check to the town of Moose Junction in order to keep the library open. The check came with a note written directly to me, which Harriet showed me one afternoon.

Abby —

Get some decent research books. The nonfiction selection is dreadful. May I suggest starting with ExtraPlanets: Looking for Life Beyond Our Solar System?

In October, the leaves were starting to change colors. The hunters came back, wearing blaze orange and shuffling out to their tree stands at 4:00 a.m. Blair was serving dinner at Gooch's, the nicest restaurant in Waukegan County, and taking online classes in English at night. She still went to therapy twice a week, and she still cried a lot, but I didn't run in my room and hide under the covers. I sat by her and braided her hair and listened to what she had to say. Jade was starting her own college application process, but she wanted to go far away—she and Mom had planned trips out east to NYU, out west to Oregon, and down south to Austin. Our little corner of Wisconsin needed to stretch a little.

I still stole all her sweatshirts. She still made fun of me for being a nerd. But something was different. I knew she would come to my rescue. She knew I was capable of telling the truth. We no longer felt like two teams; instead, we felt like one, fumbling the ball a lot but trying our hardest to work somehow. The three of us spent more time together again. We went to the library and brought huge stacks of books to the dock. We went to Gooch's, and Blair gave us a million iced tea refills. We stayed up too late, watching trashy reality TV reruns and laughing at Jade's impressions. Things had changed, like when you break a vase and glue it back together and can still run your finger over the cracks. But one night while we ate dinner, Blair asked for seconds, and Jade didn't look at her phone once, and things like that can make a girl feel invincible.

Dad even forgave me for missing the eclipse, our Big Thing that we'd planned for all summer. We went on a long drive to Chicago that fall, just me and him, and I finally told him everything: the telescope, the time capsule, Dr. Leo Lacamoire and our completed mission.

I left out the fact that Blair, Jade, and I had dug it up ages ago. That part didn't seem like it was only my story to tell.

Dad sat in silence for a few minutes as we drove through the city's downtown.

"I wish you would have told me," he said. "I feel like my girls stopped telling me the most important things." Right as he said that, we drove past the Marriott we'd stayed at while Blair auditioned for the Joffrey. It felt so long ago.

"I'm sorry," I said, and I meant it. "And I'm really, really sorry I missed the eclipse."

"I know, Abby," he said. "It's okay."

We wouldn't have a do-over on that one. Unless you're Dr. Leo Lacamoire, a total eclipse is a once-in-a-lifetime thing. But we did drive to the planetarium. We peered into the Atwood Sphere, where you can see how the night sky looked over the city in 1913. A snapshot, of how things had been then.

When my cell phone showed a number from New York one day after school, I assumed it was one of those phone calls telling you that you've won a tropical vacation or that your car insurance needed updating (I don't even have my driver's license, but I somehow got those voice mails once every few months). When I answered it, though, it was so much more.

"Is this Abigail McCourt?" a nice-sounding guy said.

"Yeah," I answered cautiously. "Who's this?"

"My name is Brent Browning. My friend Jo asked me to give you a call. She said it was a personal favor to one of her clients."

"Jo?"

"Joanna Creech?"

Joanna Creech. Power suit lady. Book editor extraordinaire. I could hardly breathe.

Brent Browning was super nice. He explained that if you wanted to get a book published, you couldn't just mail it to someone like Joanna Creech. You had to have someone called an agent send it for you, or else it would wind up in the garbage can. Besides, Joanna Creech only worked with books about science, but he told me that *his* job was to sell graphic novels to editors who wanted to place them in stores. Brent had glanced at *Planet Pirates* and said they were really well done, but not quite a story. He suggested I take a creative writing class or two in high school, try to get them formatted more clearly, and then reach out to him when I graduated.

"Look, I'm a busy guy," he said. "I don't usually chase people down. But Jo has done me a few solids, and when I saw your work, I was blown away. I can't believe you're only twelve. A few more years under your belt and some proper story structure, and I can really see you and your sister going places. You keep my phone number, okay?"

So maybe I was Going Places, too.

He told me to keep up the good work, and I promised

I would be in touch in a few years. I knew my dream of *Planet Pirates* wasn't going to save Blair. I couldn't save Blair. Jade had been right all along. Only Blair could save herself.

But it was still pretty cool to get a phone call from New York City.

Eventually, I would get a longer letter from Leo. In fact, he would eventually return to Moose Junction, almost every summer, and stay in our cabins. He would help me learn about the stars, and I would help him understand that you can't go backward. You have to move forward, just like space—always moving, changing, exploding, re-forming, and becoming new.

But we aren't at that part of the story yet.

I didn't know any of this, that night. I only knew that I had my sisters, and parents who tried really hard and loved me, and a dog who slobbered. I knew that the average galaxy contained forty billion stars. I knew that I contained stardust that connected me to everyone on the planet—my sisters, Joanna Creech, even Simone. Even Lyra Lacamoire. I knew I had nothing to fear. I knew that I was home, whatever came next.

ACKNOWLEDGMENTS

All glory to Jesus, forever and ever.

Alyssa Miele: the fact that you are right under Jesus in my acknowledgments should show you how much I value you for your honesty, attention to detail, and passion. This book is infinitely better because of your care for it! I'm also so grateful for Kathryn Silsand, Jessica White, Rosemary Brosnan, Jacquelynn Burke, and everyone else at HarperCollins who had a hand in making this book something I'm proud of.

Thank you to Alex Slater, without whom this book would be a Word doc on my computer. Your constant belief in me and my talent has made me the author I am today, and I'm so grateful for your enthusiasm and kindness. Here's to many more stupid questions.

Thank you, thank you, thank you to Pascal Campion, who designed the gorgeous book cover. You brought Abby to life in a way I could only dream of.

Multiple women shared their stories with me to make sure Blair's journey was as realistic as possible, and I am so grateful for your insight and vulnerability.

When I wanted to be an author, Kristi Weimerskirch and Angie Stanton were the ones who instantly said I could do it. I am forever grateful for your friendship.

There have been so many mornings where drinking coffee and complaining about Daniel Tiger was exactly what I needed. So thank you times infinity to Kate Lawton, Heather Bishop, Katie Steffe, Stacey Irvine, and the rest of our Wednesday crew, as well as Amanda Felsman and Leah Landrie.

This book would never have been written if Mindy Duch didn't love my children so well. Thank you for everything you do for my kiddos, Miss Mindy!

Thank you to Serena and the rest of the crew at Cafe de Arts in Sussex, Wisconsin, where this entire book was written—large light roast, please.

The listeners of the Catholic Feminist Podcast are the best supporters a girl could ask for. I see you all out there, cheering me on—thanks for listening and reading and praying!

Thank you to the entire town of Boulder Junction, Wisconsin, who welcomes my family with such open arms every summer and lets me steal a bit of its magic for my readers.

What Happens Next is frequently referred to as a

"sibling story," and I wouldn't be who I am without mine: Paul Courchane, John Courchane, Jenna Courchane, Ellen Thalacker, Cole Thalacker, and Asia Swinarska. My biggest cheerleaders, my #bestlife companions—let's go to Wittig's and celebrate. As always, the Uselman, Courchane, & Swinarski clans have inspired me and rooted for me, especially Monika and Jacek Swinarski. I am so lucky to be in the family I'm in.

To Mark and Grace Courchane: thanks for the braces, the T-ball registration forms, letting me paint my room orange, and all the other things I should have thanked you for but never did. Most of all, thank you for believing in me every single day.

Benjamin, Tess, Krzys: my very own people. I love you more than all the stars in the sky.